"You may get in," Brennan said. "But you'll never get out."

Jenny bowed her head. It didn't matter; she had to try. She had to get her son back.

"All right, damn it," he said.

Jenny's head snapped up.

"I'll do it," he said suddenly. "I'll go to Jahan, and I'll get your kid."

She put her hands over her eyes and started to cry.

"Don't do that!" he said, more sharply than he intended. "Just drink your drink and be quiet. Okay?"

"I . . . I don't know how to thank you."

"You can thank me with your sixteen thousand bucks," he said, trying to sound tough. Because he knew if he didn't, he would be sliding around the booth and putting his arms around her. And, by damn, if there was one thing he didn't need, one thing he never did, it was to start any kind of emotional attachment to a client . . . .

Dear Reader,

What a great lineup of books we have to start off your New Year. Take our American Hero, for instance. In *Cuts Both Ways,* award-winning writer Dee Holmes has created one of the most irresistible heroes you'll ever meet. Ashe Seager is a professional tracker, but the case Erin Kenyon brings to him is one he'd rather not take. Solving it will mean solving the mysteries of his own heart, and of his feelings for this woman who has haunted his memory for years.

Our Romantic Traditions miniseries continues with *Finally a Father,* by Marilyn Pappano. This is a terrific "secret baby" book! The rest of the month is equally fabulous, with new offerings from Naomi Horton (who can resist a book called *Born To Be Bad*?), Barbara Faith, Sandy Steen and Alicia Scott. You'll want to spend every evening curled up on the couch with the heroes and heroines who populate our pages this month, and I can't blame you.

So ring in the New Year the romantic way, and then make a resolution to come back next month for another taste of romance—only from Silhouette Intimate Moments.

Enjoy!

Leslie J. Wainger
Senior Editor and Editorial Coordinator

Please address questions and book requests to:
Reader Service
U.S.: P.O. Box 1325, Buffalo, NY 14269
Canadian: P.O. Box 1050, Niagara Falls, Ont. L2E 7G7

MIDNIGHT
MAN

Barbara Faith

Silhouette® INTIMATE MOMENTS®

Published by Silhouette Books

America's Publisher of Contemporary Romance

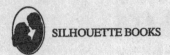 SILHOUETTE BOOKS

ISBN 0-373-07544-8

MIDNIGHT MAN

Copyright © 1994 by Barbara Faith

Printed in U.S.A.

Books by Barbara Faith

Silhouette Intimate Moments

The Promise of Summer #16
Wind Whispers #47
Bedouin Bride #63
Awake to Splendor #101
Islands in Turquoise #124
Tomorrow Is Forever #140
Sing Me a Lovesong #146
Desert Song #173
Kiss of the Dragon #193
Asking for Trouble #208
Beyond Forever #244
Flower of the Desert #262
In a Rebel's Arms #277
Capricorn Moon #306
Danger in Paradise #332
Lord of the Desert #361
The Matador #432
Queen of Hearts #446
Cloud Man #502
Midnight Man #544

Silhouette Shadows

A Silence of Dreams #13

Silhouette Special Edition

Return to Summer #335
Say Hello Again #436
Heather on the Hill #533
Choices of the Heart #615
Echoes of Summer #650
Mr. Macho Meets His Match #715
This Above All #812

Silhouette Desire

Lion of the Desert #670

Silhouette Books

Silhouette Summer Sizzlers 1988
"Fiesta!"

BARBARA FAITH

is a true romantic who believes that love is a rare and precious gift. She has an endless fascination with the attraction a man and a woman from different cultures and backgrounds have for each other. She considers herself a good example of such an attraction, because she has been happily married for over twenty years to an ex-matador she met when she lived in Mexico.

For Geneva, of course

Chapter 1

Mike Brennan walked tough, talked tough and was tough. At forty he had character lines in his forehead and a nose that had been broken more times than he wanted to remember. His face looked as though it had been through a couple of wars and at least a dozen skirmishes. Yet when he shouldered his way through the crowd that surrounded the gaming tables at the Las Vegas Casino Hotel, every woman between nineteen and eighty-nine turned to give him that special look women give a man who has, even for a moment, made them wonder what he'd be like in bed.

He was restless. Hell, he'd been restless for six months, desk bound while he sent the men who worked for him out to do the jobs he wanted to do. Unconsciously, a hand went down to rub his thigh. He walked with barely a limp now, but for a couple of months it had been touch and go. The bullet had cut through muscle and tendon before it nicked the artery. At first they hadn't been sure they could save his life, let alone his leg. He'd been barely conscious, but he still remembered screaming at the doctor in Mozambique, "Son of a bitch, you cut off my leg and you'll be talking soprano the rest of your life."

They'd saved his leg, and when he was able to travel, he'd been airlifted back to Vegas. He'd spent a month in the hospital there and was released only when he swore on a stack of Dr. Bill Cole's medical books that he'd take it easy for at least six months.

He hated inactivity. He wanted action, and since this was the only action available at the moment, he threw a twenty on a blackjack table, and stood at nineteen. He let the money ride and caught a blackjack. Before he could play again his beeper beeped.

"Damn!" he swore under his breath. It was just like Ella to call him right at the start of a winning streak. But business was business; he gathered up his winnings and headed for the nearest phone.

The only time Geneva Cooper Hurani had been in a gambling casino had been during her senior year at Santa Cruz. She and her two roommates, Josie McCall and Rosa Hernandez, had gone to Reno. She'd won sixty-five dollars on a quarter slot machine and had treated for dinner that night. It had been fun and the three of them had talked about coming back. But a few weeks later she'd met Aiden, and that had been the end of weekend outings with her friends.

With the thought of him her stomach tightened and she felt the slight hint of nausea that remembering brought. A momentary dizziness weakened her knees and she stopped to lean on one of the slot machines.

"That's my machine you're leaning on!" A gray-haired woman in red pants and a T-shirt that declared she Loved Las Vegas glowered at her from four machines away. "These are all mine," she roared. "Don't touch 'em!"

Geneva stared at her. With a shake of her head to indicate she had absolutely no interest in gambling, she moved on.

When she'd entered the hotel, she had asked at the front desk where she could find the office of Command, Inc. The desk clerk had looked her up and down before he'd said, "Go through the casino to the elevator. Take it to the top floor."

She'd looked toward the bank of elevators to the right of the desk.

"Not those," the man had said with a shake of his head. "You need to go through the casino to the private elevator."

She'd first heard about the organization from an article in the *San Diego Union-Tribune*. The story had been about a woman whose two children had been taken out of the country by her husband, a foreigner. The woman had tried every means available—the police, the FBI, the State Department—but not one had been able to help. Finally somebody had told her about an organization that went into a country undercover to try to get kidnapped children out and back to their mothers. Geneva had called the reporter who'd covered the story and he'd agreed to meet her.

"The group is headed by a man named Mike Brennan," he'd said. "The men who work with him are former Green Berets and Delta Force, men who've been in Nam or Desert Storm and who've probably been involved in covert government operations in

Central America and a lot of other places. They don't advertise what they do. The woman we did the story on learned about it from an investigative reporter in Chicago. It took her a month to try to track down the organization."

Geneva had clenched her hands together before she asked, "Did they get her children back?"

The reporter nodded. "But the man who went in was caught, slapped into prison and tortured. One of the other men in the organization got him out and then got the kids, too." He'd shaken his head. "It's a risky business, Mrs. Hurani. Command, Inc. is expensive. Maybe there's some other way."

"I've tried all the other ways," she'd said.

She had a little over sixteen thousand dollars, the six she'd gotten from selling her car and the ten she'd borrowed from her parents. She wasn't sure it was enough, but it was all she had.

"If it's more, we'll mortgage the ranch," her father had told her before she'd left San Diego County. "We'll do whatever it takes to get Timmie back."

Whatever it takes. Geneva squared her shoulders, and when she saw a cocktail waitress approach, she said, "Please, could you tell me where the elevator is?"

"Way down at the end of the casino," the young woman answered. "Behind the bandstand."

Geneva thanked her, and clutching her purse close to her chest, hurried toward the back of the convention-floor-size room. Past whirling roulette wheels, dice games and blackjack tables. Past the women and men who watched the rolling whirl of cherries and hearts and yellow lines that said Jackpot and who turned, faces tight with anger, when they heard the ringing of a bell that meant somebody else had hit it big. Past the sound of dice thudding against a table-top, the cries of, "Come *on,* seven!" Past the slap of cards at a blackjack game.

She reached the bandstand. The music was harsh and loud. No one was listening. She went around the back of it and saw the elevator. She pushed the button; the doors opened. Inside the only button read Up. She punched it with her thumb, and with the barest sensation of motion, the car zipped upward. When the doors opened, she stepped out. There were four un-marked doors along the hallway. At the end was an-other door, this one with the words Command, Inc.

She opened it.

Inside was a reception room. Gray file cabinets against one wall. Bookcases. Coffee machine. A closed door. Computer table with two computers. A fax machine. A desk with a woman behind it—brown hair, brown eyes, brown suit; late forties or early fif-ties.

The woman looked up, lowered wire-rimmed half glasses on her nose and in a no-nonsense voice asked, "Yes?"

"I..." Geneva cleared her throat. "I'm looking for a man. A—"

"Aren't we all?" With a sigh, the woman mo-tioned to the chair in front of the desk. "Sit," she said.

Geneva sat. She took a scrap of paper out of her purse. "I'm looking for a Mr. Brennan," she said. "Michael Brennan."

"Why?"

"Why?" Geneva bit her lower lip and frowned. "I read in the San Diego paper about this organization, and somebody, a reporter, told me that maybe Mr. Brennan could help me."

"How?"

Geneva stared at the other woman. Did she always speak in one-word sentences? And why did she have to look so severe, so disapproving? "My ex-husband has taken my four-year-old son out of the country. I've tried everything, every possible way to get him back, but nothing has worked. No one will help me. I read about another San Diego woman who was in the same situation. The name Command, Inc. was mentioned."

"It shouldn't have been." She shook her head. "There's no one available now. All our men are out of the country. Perhaps in a month or two—"

"No!" Geneva started up out of her chair. The room tilted. She gripped the edge of the desk, then with a strangled moan fell back against the chair and covered her eyes. "Oh, God," she whispered. "Oh, God."

The woman loomed over her. "Easy," she said, and hurried across the room. She returned with a cup of tea. "Drink," she ordered.

Geneva took a sip. "Sorry," she said. "Sorry."

"Nothing to be sorry about. What's your name?"

"Geneva, but almost everybody calls me Jenny. Jenny Cooper Hurani."

"I'm Ella Hirchberg. Hurani's your ex? The one who's got your kid?"

Jenny's eyes filled and she nodded.

"How long has it been?"

"Almost six months."

"No word from your ex?"

"No, nothing."

"What've you done, Jenny? I mean, who else have you tried?"

"The police first."

Ella Hirchberg snorted. "Who else?"

"My lawyer, the one who handled my divorce. The State Department, my congressman. I even went to the Jahanian Embassy in Washington. They turned me away."

"Figures."

"I don't know what else to do," Jenny said. "I tried going to Jahan. They wouldn't give me a visa."

"Good thing. You go in, you might never come out."

"I'm willing to take that chance. I've got to get my son." Dove gray eyes looked up at Ella Hirchberg. "You're my last chance. If you can't help me, I'll get into the country some way, somehow, by myself."

The secretary rested a lanky haunch on the edge of her desk. "Drink your tea," she said as she reached for the phone. She dialed a number, and when somebody answered, she said, sounding like a marine drill sergeant barking an order to a grunt, "Call Brennan and tell him to get his tail up here. On the double."

She hung up the phone and looked at Jenny. "We'll see," she said.

Who in the hell did Ella Hirchberg think she was? If she wasn't the best secretary in Las Vegas, and if she didn't make the best margarita in Nevada, he'd have fired her a long time ago. He was starting a winning streak and it made him mad as hell that she'd bothered him. Why? For a second he felt a moment of fear. Had something happened to one of his men? He tried to remember where they were. Juan Manuel was in

Central America, Rafe in Shanghai, Tony in Bosnia, Paco in Cuba. He shouldn't have sent Paco. Cuba was dangerous, but State had asked for help and Paco, whose father had been killed in the Bay of Pigs, had insisted he was the best man for the job. If something happened to him, to any of them . . .

He strode into the office. "What is it?" he barked. "Which one . . ." He stopped. A young woman sat at the desk across from Ella. He gave her a quick appraisal: gray eyes too big for her pale face, straight nose, tremulous mouth. Summer dress, white pumps, sheer stockings, great legs. *Nice* written all over her. And vulnerable. God, how he hated vulnerable.

He looked at Ella. "Well?" he said.

"This is Geneva," Ella said. "Geneva Cooper Hurani. Friends call her Jenny. Jenny, this is Mike Brennan."

The young woman offered her hand. He took it. It felt small and warm in his. "You wanted to see me?" he asked.

She nodded. "It's about my son."

"Your husband's got him?"

"Yes."

"Where? What country?"

"Jahan."

Brennan swore. He shot a look at Ella, as though to say it was her fault he had to deal with this. Then to Jenny he said, "Okay, come on in to my office."

His desk was a mess, cluttered with papers, books, notebooks, uncapped pens, a scattering of paper clips and chewing-gum wrappers. The chair behind it was big enough for his over-six-foot frame. He indicated the chair in front of the desk, then went around and opened a desk drawer to take out a pack of cigarettes.

"You smoke?" he asked.

Jenny shook her head.

He shook a cigarette out and rolled it around in his fingers. "Neither do I," he said.

She raised her eyebrows.

"I quit two months ago."

"Then why are you...?" She indicated the cigarette.

He shrugged. "I still like the feel of the damn thing." He crumpled it up and tossed it into the wastebasket next to the desk. "Tell me about your son. When did your husband take him?"

"Ex-husband," Jenny said.

"Okay, ex-husband. How long has it been?"

"Six months."

He fished a yellow pad out of the mess on his desk. "The boy's name?"

"Tamar Hurani. Timmie. He's almost five." She reached in her purse, took out a photograph and slid it across the desk.

Almost reluctantly, Brennan picked it up. It was a typical studio picture, taken at a Sears or a Penneys. But the boy wasn't typical. His skin was the color of golden sand and his blond hair was a mass of curls. He had her eyes. He clutched an orange giraffe in one hand and he was smiling into the camera.

Brennan studied it for a moment, then he sighed and handed it back to her. "Ex's name?"

"Aiden—Aiden Hurani. I met him at college. Santa Cruz. He's from Jahan. We were married a week after graduation."

Brennan watched her while she talked. She was twenty-eight or -nine, he thought. Small, compact body. Maybe five foot three, and a hundred and ten pounds. Silky blond hair soft around her face. An air of innocence that somehow touched him, because he could imagine what she'd looked like when she met Hurani. She'd have been about twenty-one. Virginal, inexperienced. Too young to know that it wasn't a good idea to fall for a guy from the Middle East. Once in a while that kind of a marriage worked; most of the time it didn't. It was especially dangerous if there were children, because when trouble came there was a chance the guy would go back to his own country and take his kid with him.

There were over ten thousand cases of that kind of parental kidnapping that he'd heard about. The chances of getting those kids back to their mothers were slim.

"Where're you from?" he asked.

"Ramona, California. It's near San Diego. My folks have a ranch there. Timmie and I went to live with them after the divorce."

"Tell me about your marriage. How'd it go?"

"The first few years were all right. We had some disagreements, but nothing serious. Aiden said he didn't want children right away, so we waited a couple of years before I got pregnant with Timmie. When he was two, Aiden's father and brother came from Jahan for a visit." She looked down at her hands. "That's when it started to get bad," she said.

Brennan tapped the pen on the desk top. "Brother's name?" he asked.

"Mustafa."

"The father?"

"Tamar Ben Hurani."

He wrote the names down. "Go on. What happened after they came?"

"They said Aiden had changed, that he'd forgotten the ways of his country and of his religion. They didn't approve of me or of the way Aiden was...handling me. I'd been doing volunteer teaching two days a week at a center for disturbed children. I cut back to one day a week after Timmie was born, but the work meant a lot to me. It was what I'd been trained to do. But Aiden's brother..."

Her voice trembled and he saw the fear in her eyes.

"He said—he said I shouldn't have any outside interests, so Aiden made me stop going to the center. I had to stop seeing friends. I couldn't have my next-door neighbor in for coffee. I couldn't..." She had to stop while she fought for control. "I—I couldn't even shop for groceries by myself. I had to be accompanied by either Aiden or Mustafa." She looked down at her hands. "I was a prisoner in my own home, Mr. Brennan."

"What about your parents?" he asked. "Did you tell them what the situation was?"

Jenny shook her head. "I was too embarrassed. I thought that when Aiden's father and Mustafa went back to Jahan, things would be better. But they weren't." She looked at Brennan, then away, as though ashamed. "He began to abuse me," she said in a voice so low he could barely hear. "He said I had to be punished until I learned how to act like a Jahanian wife. The beatings got worse, more frequent. He used any excuse...if a neighbor came over, if a salesman came to the door and Aiden thought I smiled at him. If his dinner wasn't ready on time."

The muscles in Brennan's shoulders tightened and bunched. He looked at the woman sitting across from him, head bowed, fair hair covering her face. He saw the splash of tears on one pale hand, and shoved his chair back.

"Let's get out of here," he said.

Jenny looked up at him, startled.

He came around the desk. "We'll have a steak. A drink. It'll make you feel better."

She swiped at her tears. "You don't have to do that."

"Yeah, I do." He took her hand and helped her to her feet. "It's almost five and I haven't eaten since breakfast."

He stood over her, almost a foot taller than she was. "When's the last time you had something to eat?"

"This morning before I left Ramona."

Still holding her hand, he led her toward the door. Ella Hirchberg looked up. "We're going out for an early dinner," he told her. "Call me at The Chop House if anything turns up."

"Okay." She looked at Jenny, then back at him and frowned.

"Wait in the hall," he told Jenny. "There's something I need to say to Miss Hirchberg."

When she had gone out and closed the door behind her, he turned to Ella. "What's your problem?" he snapped.

She stood and faced him, hands flat on the top of her desk, mouth drawn into a thin, tight line. "I'm sorry for her, too, but we don't have anybody right now who can handle a job like that."

"Sure we do."

Ella glared at him. "If you're thinking of taking it on—"

"If I am, you'll be the first to know." He turned away, careful not to limp. "Don't worry," he said over his shoulder. "I'm just going to listen to what she has to say and send her on her way."

"Sure you are!" Ella shook her head. "Dammit all, Brennan, you're in no condition—"

But he'd already gone out and closed the door behind him.

The Chop House was furnished with fine dark wood, dim lights and red leather seats. Brennan ordered two margaritas and a plate of nachos. He waited until the drinks came and Jenny had taken a sip of hers before he said, "Why didn't you go home to your parents? After he started abusing you, I mean?"

"I did, finally, but for a long time I was afraid to. Aiden told me that if I tried, he'd take Timmie away from me and I'd never see either one of them again."

Jenny took a sip of her drink and he saw that her hands were shaking.

"When I realized that the way we were living had started to affect Timmie as much as it did me, I made up my mind to leave. The company Aiden worked for sent him to Chicago for a week, and Timmie and I left and went to my folks in Ramona. That same week I filed for divorce."

"It's final?"

Jenny nodded.

"Do you have legal custody of your son?"

"Yes, but the court gave Aiden visitation rights."

Brennan swore.

"My lawyer objected, but it didn't do any good." She looked at him. "I was so afraid, Mr. Brennan. So afraid Aiden would take Timmie away."

He had a sudden and almost overwhelming urge to reach across the table and take her hand. But he didn't, he only waited.

"And one day..." For a moment she couldn't speak. When she could, she looked at Mike Brennan and said, "Please help me. I don't know where else to go. I've got sixteen thousand dollars. If it isn't enough, I'll get more. But please, please help me."

He looked at her, then away. Without thinking, he reached under the table and started to massage his leg. "The men who work for me are out on other jobs in other countries," he said.

Her eyes went bleak.

"I do mostly undercover government work. I don't take on jobs like yours."

"I see," she said, and started to slide out of the booth.

He reached out and grabbed her wrist, holding her, forcing her back into her seat. "Where're you going?" he asked. "Come on, finish your drink, okay? Then we'll have a steak—"

"I don't want a steak."

"You have to eat."

"I don't have to do anything except find my son. If you won't help me, then I'll go to Jahan myself. I've already tried that, but they said...their government said I couldn't." She looked at him, gray eyes angry and determined. "But I'll get in. Somehow I'll get in."

"You may get in," Brennan said. "But you'll never get out."

Jenny bowed her head. That was the same thing Ella Hirchberg had said. It didn't matter; she had to try. She had to get her son back.

"All right, dammit," Brennan said.

Jenny's head snapped up.

"I'll do it." He downed most of his margarita. "I'll go to Jahan and I'll get your kid."

She put her hands over her eyes and started to cry.

"Don't do that!" he said, more sharply than he intended. "Just drink your drink and be quiet. Okay?"

"I—I don't know how to thank you."

"You can thank me with your sixteen thousand bucks," he said, trying to sound tough. If he didn't, he'd be sliding around the booth and putting his arms around her. And by damn, if there was one thing he didn't need, one thing he never did, it was to start any kind of emotional attachment to a client.

Chapter 2

He wasn't sure why he'd agreed to take her case. God knows it wasn't for the money, because the sixteen thousand wouldn't even begin to cover what it would cost. Besides the airline tickets, there'd be hefty bribes getting into Jahan and heftier ones getting out. If he got out.

So why had he said he'd do it? Maybe because he was tired of being inactive and because he needed to prove to himself that Mozambique hadn't spooked him. Or maybe it was because when she'd looked at him, he'd seen the gut-deep despair in her eyes.

Geneva. He liked her name. But he liked Jenny, too. It was an innocent, childlike name and it suited her. Maybe in another five or ten years she'd look like a Geneva, but for now she was simply Jenny.

Hirchberg, when he'd told her he was going to Jahan, had called him a damn fool. "Let Rafe handle it when he gets back," she'd said. "He's your num-

ber-one man in the Middle East. Your leg's still both-
ering you. You're out of shape.''

"I'll get back into shape."

It wouldn't take much, he told himself. A couple of
weeks in the desert to work off the flab, get the muscles toned, the breath back. Run himself hard with a
fifty-pound pack, get in some target practice, sleep out
under the stars again.

Last night, when he'd taken Jenny Hurani back to
her hotel, they'd agreed to meet this morning for
breakfast to talk things over. He wanted every scrap of
information he could get on the Hurani family, everything her ex might have told her about them, about
how they lived and where they lived. He needed to pick
her memory, to find out anything she'd ever heard
about Aiden's life in Jahan.

But first he had to get in touch with Kumar.

Kumar Ben Ari, son of royal blood. The bravest
man he'd ever known, fiercely independent in spite of
his family's great wealth.

Mike had met Kumar in Saudi Arabia during the
last days of Desert Storm. Neither of them had been
there in an official capacity, but the undercover jobs
they'd been assigned had brought them together in
Saudi, Kuwait and Iraq. By the time the mop-up operations were under way, they'd completed the job
they'd been sent to do. And they'd become friends.
When Kumar invited him to spend a few weeks at his
vacation home in Jahan, he'd accepted.

Although he wasn't from that country, Kumar kept
a home there because of his oil interests. The first time
Mike had seen it, he'd thought, *Not only is Kumar a
prince, damned if he doesn't live like one.* The palace, for that's what it was, was something out of the

Arabian Nights. But then, so was Kumar. The three weeks Brennan spent with his friend in Jahan were the best he remembered in a long time. They'd ridden Kumar's magnificent Arabian steeds at breakneck speed over the desert dunes. They'd camped out with Bedouins and fought a minor desert skirmish.

And when they'd returned to the palace in the capital city, they'd wined and dined and romped with their share of sloe-eyed dancing girls, who in addition to their other talents had helped ensure Mike's fluency in Jahanian.

Kumar was a brave and fearless friend. He had told Brennan before he left that if Brennan ever needed him, all he had to do was call.

So Mike called. "I'm coming in," he said. "I'll need help."

"I'm at your service, my friend. You have only to tell me what I am to do."

Mike told him about Jenny Hurani, and that he was coming to Jahan to get her son.

Kumar whistled. "It won't be easy, Mike. The Huranis are a rich and powerful family. I can help you up to a point, but I'm not a Jahanian. If you're caught there will be great danger. You must be aware of that."

"I'm aware," Mike said.

He told Kumar it would be at least three weeks before he could get things together. "If I can't get a visa, I'll have to come in some other way. I'll let you know."

"The dancing girls will be happy to hear that you are returning," Kumar said before he hung up.

Mike grinned when he put the phone down. He reached for a cigarette and rolled it back and forth between his fingers a couple of times, held it up to his nose and sniffed the tobacco, then with a mild curse tossed it into the wastebasket.

The next morning, over scrambled eggs with enough hot sauce to cure every disease known to man, he told Jenny what he'd told Kumar—that it would take at least three weeks to get things lined up before he left for Jahan. "I figure I can get out of here by the first of next month."

"Of course, I'm going with you," she said.

His face went still. He glared at her. "The hell you are!"

She looked across the table at him, eyes level, small chin set and defiant. "Timmie is my son," she said. "He's been through the trauma of being taken away from me. For the past six months he's lived among strangers in an atmosphere completely foreign to him. How do you think he'll feel when a strange man suddenly appears to snatch him away?"

She leaned across the table, her gaze steady. "He's a little boy, Mr. Brennan. I have to be there when you rescue him. I have to reassure him, to let him know that everything is going to be all right."

"It's out of the question, Mrs. Hurani. I won't even discuss it."

"I can tell you things about the family you need to know."

"You can tell me without coming with me."

"Aiden told me all about the house, enough so that I think I could find my way around it blindfolded."

"Draw me a diagram."

"I can speak enough of the language to get by," she went on, as though she hadn't heard him. "I may have acted like a wimp yesterday, but I'm not a wimp. I'm

stronger than I look and healthy as a horse. I won't
whine or complain and I won't run scared if things get
dangerous. I can ride and I'm a good shot."

Brennan leaned back in his chair. "You ever shoot
a man?" he asked.

Her eyes widened. "Of course not!"

"What if you had to?"

"I don't know the answer to that," she said truth-
fully. "I think I could if it meant protecting Timmie." She gave a lopsided smile. "But I'd aim for an
arm or a leg."

Brennan didn't smile back. "This isn't television,"
he said. "You shoot, you shoot to kill. It isn't fun or
games or let's pretend. The man who went after the
kids of the woman you read about was captured.
When we got him out of the local prison, he couldn't
walk, because the bottoms of his feet had been so
badly burned. When he got back here he spent two
months in the hospital having skin grafts."

Jenny looked down at her coffee cup. "I realize
there'll be danger," she said.

"Danger!" Mike snorted. "Lady, you don't even
know the meaning of the word."

"Maybe I don't, Mr. Brennan. But nothing you can
say will stop me. I *am* going to Jahan with you."

"No, little lady, you are not."

He argued with her until his face turned red and he
was ready to leap across the table and shake the living
hell out of her. She wouldn't budge. He told her every
horror story he could remember of men who had gone
unwelcome into foreign countries and been captured
and tortured. He told them in graphic detail. Her face
paled but she held onto her determination. He tossed
her check back at her and said the deal was off. She

said she'd go in by herself if he didn't go with her. Finally he threw up his hands and said, "All right! All right! You can go under one condition."

She smiled. "What's that, Mr. Brennan?"

"You do exactly what I say. You do whatever I tell you to do."

"Of course, Mr. Brennan."

"And you will by God stop calling me Mr. Brennan. My name is Mike. Got that?"

"Got it," she said. "Why do we have to wait so long? Why can't we leave tomorrow?"

Now it was his turn to smile. "Because, Miss Jenny, I'm going to take you out into the desert and get you in shape before we leave. I'm going to march you up one sand dune after another. I'm going to strap a twenty-five-pound pack on your back and make you run five miles through the sand. I'm going to teach you how to defend yourself."

The smile faded and his expression hardened. "I'll treat you like you're a new recruit and I'm a drill sergeant. You yell 'uncle' and the deal's off. Is that clear?"

Jenny looked at him. Then, squaring her shoulders, she gave a salute. "Yes, *sir!*" she barked. "Anything you say, *sir!*"

And the deal was done.

Jenny took a bus to Ramona to tell her folks what she was going to do. On her return, Brennan picked her up in L.A. and took her to a sporting-goods store, where he outfitted her in fatigues, a wide-brimmed hat and heavy boots.

"What about sneakers?" she said with a frown. "The boots weigh about ten pounds each."

"I know, but they'll work out fine when you're running through the desert." He clenched his jaw to keep from laughing. A day of running with a pack on her back in 114° heat and she'd be yelling for mercy. Once she did, he'd get on with the job he had to do.

They packed their supplies, bedrolls, guns and ammo into his Jeep, and before dawn on a Monday morning in May, left Las Vegas for Death Valley Junction.

"Death Valley?" Jenny asked. "That's the hottest spot in the country."

"Yep." He shot her a glance. "We'll leave the Jeep at the Junction and walk in."

Jenny glanced at the back of the Jeep. "That's a lot of stuff to carry," she murmured.

"Uh huh." Brennan looked straight ahead and tried to hide his smile. A day of walking in the sun and she'd be ready to call it quits.

He drove to a small motel he knew. They had breakfast and he talked to the owner about leaving the Jeep there.

"Sure thing, Mike," Gus Crocket said. "How long you gonna be gone?"

"Two weeks. Maybe longer."

Gus took his straw hat off and scratched his head. "It'll be hotter'n spit on a griddle," he said.

"Yeah, probably."

Gus looked at Jenny. "You spend much time in the desert, little lady?"

"No." Jenny cleared her throat and forced a smile. "First time."

Mike clapped a hand on her shoulder. "She's healthy as a horse," he said, mimicking her words.

"And looking forward to it." He grinned down at her. "Aren't you, honey?"

She shot him an if-looks-could-kill glance and said, "You bet I am."

He hoisted a pack out of the Jeep and strapped it on her back. "How's that?" he asked when he'd adjusted the straps.

"Fine," she said. "Just fine."

"Not too heavy?"

She shook her head. What had he put in it? Gold bricks?

He took a bedroll out of the Jeep and tied it above her pack, then slung a rifle and a bandolier of bullets over her head.

She staggered under the weight.

"Too much?" he asked.

"No, no, it's..." She grunted, trying to keep her balance. "It's fine," she said.

"Then we're all set. See you in a couple of weeks, Gus."

"Sure you don't want to go on over to Sam's place and rent a mule?" the old man asked.

"Don't need a mule when I've got Miss Jenny here." Brennan hefted his own pack and slung another rifle over his shoulder. He smiled at her. "Come on, woman," he said. "Let's go."

Three hours went by. When they first started out, they'd seen an occasional Jeep or Land Rover. Once Mike pointed out an old mine shaft and a couple of beehive-shaped charcoal kilns. But for the last hour there'd been nothing. Only rocks, dry, cracked earth and sand, with an occasional patch of sage or sandpaper plants.

The straps cut into Jenny's shoulders. The boots weighed a ton, the pack two tons. Sweat ran down her back and between her breasts.

Brennan whistled while he walked. Every time she looked at him he smiled, as though to say, "My, isn't this fun?"

After what seemed like half a century, he pointed into the distance. "There's shelter up ahead," he said. "We'll be there in half an hour or so."

Half an hour? Half a lifetime. She sloughed on, knees wobbly, back killing her, throat so dry she was spitting cotton.

It was little more than a shack. Outside there was a wooden awning with a table and a couple of chairs under it. Inside was a woman with a sun-wrinkled face and a shock of frizzled red hair.

"Hey, you old son of a gun!" she cried when she saw Mike. "How in the hell are ya?"

"Just fine, Gert. How've you been?"

"Can't complain." She looked at Jenny. "Lord God," she said. "You're redder'n a lobster."

"This is Jenny," Mike said. He helped her off with the pack. "Tired?" he asked. "Heat getting to you?"

"I'm a little warm," she admitted, and tried not to wince when she moved her shoulders and flexed her sore muscles. She even managed a smile when she said, "But I'm fine. Just fine."

"There's a ladies' room out back," Gert said. "It's kinda primitive but we got well water. That'll cool you off some. You're awful flushed."

Flushed! Her whole body was on fire. Jenny nodded to Gert and walked stiff legged around to the back of the shack. As the woman said, it was primitive. She ran water into a cracked basin, took off the khaki hat and splashed the water over her face. Then she rolled up her shirtsleeves and rinsed her hands and arms.

Still dripping, she leaned her hands on the sink. This was going to be tougher than she had ever imagined anything could be. She knew Mike Brennan was testing her, waiting for her to give up and admit she wasn't in any kind of shape to do this.

Maybe she wasn't, but she was darned if she'd give up. If she did, he wouldn't let her go to Jahan with him. She'd do whatever she had to do—climb every damn sand dune in the desert, carry whatever load she had to carry, lick his damn boots if he said so. But she was, by God, going with him to Jahan and there wasn't anything he could do to stop her.

She looked at her reflection in the cracked mirror. "Okay," she said. "We can do this. Right?" She nodded at the mirror and answered her own question. "Yes, we can!"

Then she took a deep breath and went back outside.

Brennan was sitting at the table outside, drinking a beer with the red-haired woman. "It's warm but it's wet," he said. "Want one?"

"No, thanks. I'd rather have a glass of water."

"Sure thing," Gert said. "I'll get it for you." She went inside, and when she came out, handed a glass to Jenny.

Jenny took a sip. It tasted like a rusty tin can, like the way a dentist's office smells. She said, "Yetch."

Mike leaned back in his chair, enjoying her reaction. "Most of the water, when we find it, will taste the same." He finished the last of his beer and handed Gert a five dollar bill.

"Good to see you again," he said. Then he picked up his pack and, when he'd strapped it on, picked up Jenny's and slipped it onto her shoulders.

She barely managed to stifle a groan, and had a terrible urge to smack him hard when he said in a cheerful tone, "Okay, partner, let's hit the trail."

Trail? There wasn't any trail. There was only an ocean of sand for as far as she could see. They plodded on, mile after endless mile, up one sand dune and down another. And all the time he whistled.

He kept waiting for her to tell him she couldn't go on, that it was too much, that she couldn't stand the heat. But she said nothing; she just kept walking. Her face was flushed and her fatigues were wet with perspiration, but she wasn't giving in.

He let her rest for ten minutes every hour. And finally, afraid she might pass out, he pointed ahead to an overhang of rocks where a few scrub palms and saguaro cactus grew and said, "Let's call it a day."

"Don't do it on my account," she muttered.

His lips twitched, but he didn't say anything.

They took their backpacks off. He found big stones, laid them in a V, arranged some twigs and a few sticks and started a fire. When it caught, he poured water from a canteen into a coffeepot, opened an envelope and poured in some coffee. In another pot he put water on to boil.

"Is this where we're going to camp while we're in the desert?" Jenny asked.

Mike shook his head. "No, but if we keep up a pretty good pace we should reach it by tomorrow afternoon. Six or seven hours ought to do it."

Six or seven hours? Jenny stifled a groan. Another hour of this and she would have been flat on her face. How could she stand another day?

She sat down and pulled off her boots and the heavy socks. Her feet were red and she had a blister on the side of her big toe.

Mike reached into his pack and pulled out a first-aid kit. "Better put a bandage on it," he said.

She nodded her thanks, wishing there was a big pool of water where she could bathe. After she'd put the bandage on she leaned back against one of the palms.

"You can unpack the bedrolls and put them down," Mike said just as she closed her eyes.

This time she couldn't stifle the groan. But she crawled to her feet, untied the bedrolls and spread them out. The coffee started to perk; the water began to boil. Brennan opened a package of dry soup mix and threw it in.

Soup? She was hungry enough to eat half a cow.

He filled two mugs with the soup and handed her a hard roll. "Your turn to cook tomorrow," he said.

She tried not to glower.

The soup was good. She ate all of it and two of the rolls. The coffee smelled good. She'd always been persnickety about drinking only decaf because she thought the caffeine would keep her awake. But tonight nothing would. She drank two cups, yawned again and again, and did her best to keep her eyes open.

"Care for a walk?" Brennan asked. "A little after-dinner stroll?"

A stroll? He had to be kidding. It was all she could do to make it from the camp fire to the bedroll.

"I'll pass," she said.

Brennan nodded. "Think I'll take a turn around." He smiled at her disbelief and set out into the darkness. And tried not to laugh when he heard her groan. She was tired and sore now, but it would be worse tomorrow. He could only imagine how much her muscles hurt, her back and her feet. He regretted having pushed so hard, but he'd done it purposefully, hoping against hope that she'd give up. But she hadn't.

The night was as clear as only a night in the desert could be. There was a sliver of new moon and a half a zillion stars. He slapped his pockets and wished he had a cigarette.

He thought about the photograph he'd seen of Jenny's son. Timmie, little boy lost, so far away from his mother. He had an uncomfortable feeling that Jenny wouldn't give in, that she'd go on until she dropped if it meant getting to her boy.

His face, shadowed by the moon, hardened. He didn't want her with him. He'd run her ragged if he had to, but before these two weeks were over he'd have her crying for mercy and yelling "Uncle!" at the top of her lungs.

He looked through the darkness at the small flicker of flames from the fire and started back. When he reached the camp he saw that she was asleep, curled up, one hand under her cheek, the fair hair loose about her face.

He looked down at her, and for the slightest fraction of a moment he felt something soften within him. Then he turned away and lay down on his bedroll.

But it was a long time that night before Mike Brennan went to sleep.

Chapter 3

"Up and at 'em. It's after five. Get a move on."

Jenny buried her face in the bedroll. "Go 'way," she mumbled.

Mike wafted a mug of coffee under her nose.

"Dark," she said. "Gotta sleep."

He sat on his haunches beside her. "Woman, if you're not out of the sack by the time I count to ten, I'm going to haul your rear end out and make you carry a double load all day. One, two..."

Jenny opened her eyes. "I could learn to really hate you," she muttered.

"Three..."

"All right!" She sat up and reached for the mug of coffee. Her hair was tousled. Her eyes were sleepy and her cheeks were red. He thought she looked about ten years old.

He stood. "Shake it up. I want to leave before the sun comes up."

"I'm hungry."

"I'll rustle up some grub while you take care of whatever it is you need to take care of."

Jenny looked around, made a face and said, "I don't see any handy public restroom."

He jerked a thumb toward the saguaro cactus. "The facilities," he said.

She gave him a killing look, then picked up the small cloth bag that held her hairbrush, toothbrush, sunscreen and lipstick. And stood up. Or tried to. Before she could stop herself, she moaned aloud with pain. Every muscle was sore. Her back felt as though she'd been beaten with a two-by-four and she could barely move her legs.

"You'll feel better when we start walking," Mike said. "That'll work the soreness out."

"Sure it will." With as much dignity as she could muster, hobbling as if she was eighty years old, Jenny headed for the cactus. When she returned, Mike handed her an apple and a dish of granola.

"This is breakfast?" she asked.

"Yep. Enjoy, but don't take too long."

Five minutes later he said, "Okay, that's it. Let me help you with your pack."

Helping meant hoisting it onto her back. Then the bedroll and the rifle.

"All set?" he asked.

She took a deep breath, managed a smile and said, "Lead on."

It was worse than yesterday. Her body screamed for help. She wanted to beg Mike Brennan to stop. Take me back, she longed to say. I can't stand the heat. I hurt all over. Every step is killing me. I can't hack it, I give up.

But every time she wanted to cry uncle, she thought about Timmie. One step for Timmie. Another step for Timmie. His name became a litany in her mind, a silent, repetitive chant. Timmie. Timmie. Timmie. She was getting stronger for him. So that she could go to him. So that she could bring him back where he belonged.

Hang on, baby, she thought. Mama's coming. Mama's coming, Timmie.

When they stopped for lunch, she couldn't eat. She lay back with her head against her pack and closed her eyes. Mike Brennan knelt on the sand beside her and held a canteen to her lips.

"A couple of more hours and we'll reach the place where we're going to camp," he said. "You can make it."

"Damn right I can," she answered without opening her eyes.

He looked down at her and a strange expression came across his face. Her own was flushed, her lips dry and blistered. He knew that every step was agony. He'd driven her at a forced march, making her keep up, hoping she'd give up. But she hadn't. He admired her for that, but he still wanted to break her, because he was damned if he'd let her go to Jahan with him.

Nevertheless, when it was time to move on, he put her bedroll over his and her rifle around his shoulders. When she protested, he said bluntly, "I'm being practical. If you can't go on, I'll end up carrying you, too."

"It'll never happen, Brennan." She shot him an angry look and started walking.

Her anger helped. She called him names under her breath and told herself he was a brute, a bum. A ma-

cho man who wanted to keep her from going after her
son. If she couldn't measure up, that's what he'd do.
She had to prove to him that she was woman enough,
strong enough to face any obstacle that lay ahead.

She gritted her teeth. One step at a time, she told
herself. That's all it takes—one step at a time.

And at last, five hours after they'd started out, they
made camp. It wasn't a desert oasis, but there was an
overhang of rocks, a few scrub trees, some cactus and
a water hole.

Mike pitched a small tent. "For the supplies," he
told Jenny. "In case of a windstorm, they'll be protected." He looked at her. Her hair hung in damp
tangles about her sweaty face. Her clothes were
stained.

"How'd you like a bath?" he asked, and handed
her a collapsible bucket and a bar of soap. "You can
bathe while I take a look around."

As soon as he disappeared over one of the dunes,
Jenny ripped her clothes off, held them at arm's length
and made a face. Then she lowered the bucket into the
water hole, drew it up and poured it over her head.
Good. Oh, damn, it felt so good she grunted with
pleasure. She scrubbed her hair, then her body. With
a towel wrapped around her, she drew another buck-
etful and rinsed. When the air had dried her, she put
on a pair of shorts and a T-shirt.

When Brennan returned he looked at her, nodded
approvingly and said, "My turn. You can put the
supplies away while I clean up."

Jenny turned away and got busy putting their food
in some kind of order. It was mostly dehydrated
stuff—food packets of chicken and rice, potatoes and

meat, lima beans and ham, powdered eggs. A lot of granola, dried fruit, fresh apples, coffee.

She could hear him drawing up more water. She darted a quick look his way and saw the pile of his clothes on the sand.

She wondered how he looked naked. Good, she thought. Probably very good. His thick black hair would be sleek with water that would drip down over his broad shoulders, his chest and muscular arms. His legs were muscled, too, and his belly was flat. She bet he had great buns....

Good Lord! She stopped, surprised and shocked at her speculation, because she hadn't thought that way about a man in more than two years. She hadn't dated, hadn't wanted anything to do with a man. Yet here she was, wondering what Mike Brennan looked like naked. It must be the heat; it had addled her brain.

When at last he said, "All set," Jenny turned around. He, too, wore shorts, and an unbuttoned denim shirt. She'd been right—his legs were long and straight and muscled. His black hair was shiny with water, and he'd shaved. He wasn't exactly handsome, but he was so damned masculine she had the sudden urge to run for cover.

"Finished unpacking?" he asked.

"Uh, yes."

"Good, then let's start supper. What'll it be? Hobo stew?"

"Fine."

"Dig out a package."

She did. It didn't look appetizing. He started a fire, put water on to boil and dumped the package in. Two weeks of this? Jenny thought with chagrin.

He tossed her an apple. "That's your appetizer," he said.

His leg ached. He wished he had a cigarette and a drink. Something tall and cool, a gin and tonic, maybe. Or rum and Coke. He gave himself a mental shake. No cigarettes or booze until this camping trip was over and he was back in shape.

He looked at Jenny across the fire. There were dark circles of fatigue under her eyes, but she looked better than she had earlier today. Good in shorts. Nice, trim little body, great legs. He started to wonder what she'd be like in bed, and brought himself up short. Whoa, Brennan, he told himself. This is strictly business. Just another case. You're here to get both of you in shape. She'll poop out, then you go to Jahan alone and get her kid. That's all. She's a client, nothing more. So don't go looking at her legs or thinking that she isn't wearing a bra. Forget it, man. She's off-limits.

But he kept watching her across the fire that night. She cleaned up her plate of stew and sopped the juice up with a hardtack biscuit. Then she got sleepy and started yawning over her coffee. When her head nodded, he took the mug out of her hand and said, "You'd better get some sleep."

"Maybe." She stood up and stretched. He saw the rise of her breasts and the small nub of her nipples pressing against the T-shirt.

She said, "G'night," kicked off the sandals she'd put on after her bath and lay down. In maybe five and a half seconds she was asleep and giving off a sort of purring snore.

He sat by the fire, arms around his bent legs, watching her through the flames. She was a small

woman, with fine skin and delicate bones. Asleep and
with her hair tumbling about her face, she looked
young and vulnerable.

He thought of what she'd said about her husband
beating her. How could a man do that to a woman?
Say, a man of his size and weight. How could he bat-
ter a woman who was smaller, defenseless? What kind
of a man would do that?

His piercing blue eyes narrowed. He swore under his
breath, and decided that before he left Jahan, he'd
arrange a few minutes alone with her husband and give
him a couple of lessons on how to act with a woman.

He looked down at his hands. Without realizing it,
he'd doubled them into fists. Cut it out, he told himself, you're taking this personally. You never get involved with a client. Remember?

But when he looked at Jenny, it was hard to remember that.

He got her up at dawn the next morning. Before
breakfast he had her out and running up one dune and
down the next. By the time they returned to camp her
face was red and her T-shirt was soaked with sweat.

He set her to boiling water and making coffee while
he rustled up some powdered eggs and dehydrated
potatoes. When the food was ready, he scooped a big
helping onto her plate. She ate like a mule skinner.

"Do you always eat this much?" he asked with a
grin.

Jenny frowned and shook her head. "You've run
me ragged, Brennan. I'm just trying to keep up my
strength. What do we do after breakfast, strap on our
packs and climb a couple of mountains?"

"That comes after lunch." He finished eating and put his plate aside. "Right now we're going to do a little target practice. You told me before that you were a good shot. Let's see how good you are."

He handed her one of the rifles. "Ever handle an M-16?"

Jenny shook her head. "Only a hunting rifle."

"This is a lot more gun." He walked out a hundred yards or so and set up separate piles of rocks with sticks pointing straight up. When he came back to her, he said, "Fire when ready."

She lifted the gun to her shoulder and sighted. The stock barely recoiled against her shoulder. She took the tops off three out of six sticks.

It was better than he expected, but it wasn't good enough.

For the next two hours he kept her shooting. When she hit six out of six he let her rest. "We'll do it again later," he said. "Tomorrow we'll see what you can do with a handgun. Now I want to see how well you can defend yourself."

During the next hour Jenny was on her back more than she was on her feet. She'd taken a self-defense course in college, but nothing she knew had prepared her for what Mike Brennan put her through. He flipped her on her back, he dropped her on her knees. He tripped her and tossed her, and there wasn't a damn thing she could do about it. Bruises added to her sore muscles, and when she finally crawled into her bedroll that night, she could barely move.

The next morning he filled her pack with rocks and chased her up and down the sand dunes. After breakfast he taught her how to fire, load and clean a 9 mm automatic. That afternoon he ran her a good three miles and when they got back to camp, there were more self-defense lessons.

She thought after that she'd be too tired to eat, but she wasn't. The dehydrated ham and lima beans were just about the most tasteless meal she'd ever had, but it didn't matter. She cleaned her plate with a piece of hard bread and asked for more. She ate it all and was just about to ask for an apple when she fell asleep.

A week went by. Every day was a repetition of the day before. Her muscles stopped hurting, but the bruises stayed. And finally, one afternoon during the self-defense lessons, she had Brennan on his knees yelling "uncle." When that happened she gave a hoot of sheer glee. After that she welcomed whatever he could teach her.

She was learning; she was getting tougher. A couple of times, even with the pack of rocks she carried on her back, she beat him to the top of a dune.

She ate everything he put on her plate, and at night she slept as though she'd been poleaxed.

At first they didn't talk a lot, at least about anything personal. But little by little Jenny began to tell him more about herself. She talked about growing up on the ranch in Ramona, and it was obvious she had a good relationship with both her parents.

"My mother's the best cook in California," she bragged. "She makes a chocolate soufflé that's pure heaven." Her father, in addition to raising cattle, was a vet. "The best in San Diego County." She smiled. "They're great people. I hope someday you'll be able to meet them."

"Yeah," he said. "So do I."

"What about you?" she asked. "Where were you raised, Mike?"

"On a mean street on the south side of Chicago. My mother was a kindergarten teacher, my father was the neighborhood drunk." He looked away from her. "He finally drank himself to death about five years ago."

That stopped her. She didn't know what to say. She took a sip of her coffee, then asked, "And your mother?"

"She died when I was twelve."

"I'm sorry, Mike."

"Yeah, so am I." He got up and went to stand with his back to her, wishing he hadn't dug up these painful memories, wondering why he had.

"A state agency took me away from my dad when I was fourteen," he said. "They put me in a foster home in Elmhurst. I was lucky, because they placed me with good people. I made the high-school football team and got a four-year football scholarship to the University of Illinois."

"What about your father?" Jenny asked. "Did you ever see him?"

"Only when he wanted to hit me up for some cash." Brennan shrugged. "I had no use for him," he said. "He was my old man, but I hated his guts."

She wanted to go to him, wanted to take his hand and tell him she was sorry. But she didn't; she only waited.

"I enlisted after college," he said. "Saw some action in the last days of Viet Nam and decided that was what I was suited for. After that I did some undercover government work, then I got into what I'm doing now. I do occasional jobs for other governments if I happen to agree with their politics. Otherwise I won't touch 'em." He walked back to Jenny. "I've only taken a couple of cases like yours," he said.

"Did you..." She was almost afraid to ask. "Did you get the children out?"

"Yes."

She let out the breath she didn't even know she'd been holding. "Where?" she asked. "What countries?"

"One was in Iran. The other one was Central America." He looked at her. "I went in alone," he said. "I didn't have a mother hanging on my shirttails."

"Then this time will be different, won't it?" She got up and moved toward him. Looking him square in the eye, she said, "This time you *will* have a mother with you. But I won't be hanging on your shirttails, Brennan. I'll be doing everything I can to help."

He glared down at her. With a shake of his head, he said, "I think you're one hell of a woman, Miss Jenny. You're tougher than I thought you'd be and you've stood up under what I've been making you do. You're a good shot and a good sport. But you're a woman, and what's worse, you're emotionally involved. That makes you a bad risk. I'm going to do my damnedest to get your boy out of Jahan, but I honest-to-God think you should let me go in alone."

Jenny shook her head. "I'm going," she said. "That's final."

He worked her even harder after that, and though there were times she faltered, she never gave up. Her skin turned brown, her muscles firmed. She could carry a fifty-pound pack without a sign of strain and run up a sand dune without panting. In spite of himself he was proud of her.

On their last night in camp they sat close to the camp fire. The moon was full, blotting out some of the stars. The air smelled clean and fresh. He broke out a bottle of Scotch, said, "One for the road," and handed it to her.

She drank and handed it back. "Tomorrow we start back?" she asked.

Brennan nodded.

"Then what?"

"It depends on a friend of mine in Jahan."

He told her about Kumar then, but didn't tell her that, if she refused to be left behind when he left the States, he was planning to stash her in the palace while he went after the boy.

"I can get into the country without too much trouble," he said, "but I'm not sure you can. You said you'd tried to get a visa?"

Jenny nodded. "They wouldn't give me one."

"Then we'll have to get phony passports." He thought for a minute. "It'd be better if we go in as a couple." He hesitated. "How do you feel about being Mrs. Mike—" he hesitated "—O'Brien?"

"How do we arrange this—this marital status?"

"I'll take care of it. We'll get you a dark wig and glasses and maybe pad you a little bit to disguise your figure, because we don't want those Jahanian dudes staking out a claim."

"You don't need to worry," she said with a frown. "I've had enough of Jahanian men to last me a couple of lifetimes."

"Yeah, I suppose you have." Then—he didn't know why—he asked, "Is that true for other men as well?"

She looked at him, startled. "I—I don't know, Mike. I think that after you've had a really bad, a really frightening relationship, you're not anxious to get into another one. I'm afraid that if a man looked at me with a leer in his eyes, I'd head for the hills. Marriage to Aiden left me gun-shy. I don't want to get hurt that way again."

She hesitated for a few moments, debating, then said, "Once, after I'd left Aiden and gone back to the ranch, my dad and I were arguing. It wasn't anything important—something about one of the horses, I think—but in the midst of the argument he raised his hand to make a point, probably to wag his finger at me. I backed away and I started shaking and saying, 'Don't hit me! Don't hit me.'" She looked down at her hands. "That's the only time I've ever seen my father cry."

Mike swore under his breath.

In a couple of minutes she said, "Something happened to me that night, Mike. I'd been afraid for a long time, but I suddenly knew I'd never be afraid again. If anybody ever lays a hand on me, I'll whop it off."

"Good for you." He tried to make his voice sound hearty, but it came out soft because the thought of her fear, and of the reason for her fear, had him all churned up inside.

But the churning stopped when she asked, "How about you? Have you ever been married?"

"Me?" He shook his head. "I've got itchy feet and a wandering eye, Miss Jenny. I'd make a terrible husband."

"One thing for sure, you'd never coddle the lady. I can hear you now, 'It's five-thirty, woman. Get out of that bed and rustle me up some grub. Tote that barge and lift that bale. Carry the piano up to the third floor, and when you've finished with that, take the refrigerator down to the basement.'"

"Aw, c'mon." He started to laugh. "I'm not that bad."

She laughed, too. "Simon Legree in khaki fatigues," she chortled. "Chasing me up one dune and down another."

"And sometimes wishing I could catch you." He stopped laughing and drew in his breath. "I wonder what you'd have done if I had. If you'd have whopped me or..." He stood abruptly and moved away from the fire. "It's getting late," he said. "We'd better get some sleep."

"I—yes, I..." She was trying hard to keep her voice steady. "I suppose we'll be leaving at dawn."

He shook his head. "I thought I'd let you sleep in a little while in the morning."

"Gee, Brennan," she said, getting up and moving toward him, "you're getting soft."

"Right." He looked at her. She was smiling. Moonlight touched her face and turned her hair to gold. Before he knew that he was going to, he reached out and rested a hand on her hair. It was silky soft under his fingers. He slid his hand down and cupped the back of her neck. It felt small, fragile.

She looked up at him, her eyes wide, her lips parted. But she didn't move away.

He kissed her, his lips little more than a brush against hers before he let her go and stepped back a pace. When she didn't move away, he put his arms around her and drew her close, and this time he kissed her the way he'd wanted to since maybe the first time she'd walked into his office in Vegas.

Whoa, she told herself. Hey, wait a minute. What're we doing? This isn't a good idea. It isn't... She put her hands flat against his chest to push him away. But didn't.

His lips were soft, yet firm against hers. And warm, oh, so warm. He tasted her, as though he were sampling her lips and liking what he sampled. He explored the corners of her mouth with his tongue. She felt a shiver of pleasure, and when he moved his tongue to find hers, she touched her own to his. And heard the whisper of pleasure deep in his throat.

She didn't remember ever having been kissed like this before. It weakened her knees; it made her want more.

He pressed a hand against the small of her back to bring her closer. She tensed, a little fearful of what he might do if she responded, and tried to draw away. He didn't try to hold her, but neither did he stop kissing her. His mouth was warm, it gave so much pleasure, and without even being aware that she did, she moved nearer.

His body was strong, masculine against her own feminine form. She felt overwhelmed by him, wrapped in his arms, feeling the hard line of his hip, the length of his leg.

"We shouldn't do this," she whispered against his mouth.

"I know."

He drew her closer still, cupping her head, bringing it to rest against his shoulder, and a shudder ran through him. He gripped her arms for a minute and then he let her go.

"Sorry," he said. "Sorry. Put it down to the Scotch, and maybe the moon."

Jenny looked up at him. "Yes," she whispered. "It was the moon." Her mouth was soft, her eyes luminous.

"Jenny..." He shook his head. "Don't look at me like that, Jenny. Because if you do..." He shook his head and stepped back two paces. "Go to bed," he said. "I'm going for a walk."

Before she could answer, he turned and walked away into the darkness. She stood there, looking after him.

"Brennan," she whispered.

And his name was a sigh of wonder on her lips.

Chapter 4

She felt the sun on her face and lay half asleep, half awake, thinking how it had been last night when Mike Brennan kissed her. She remembered other kisses: her first kiss, from Junior Hardy when she was fourteen; he'd had freckles, cowlicky hair, and he'd been more nervous than she had been. Later college dates and college kisses. And Aiden.

She had been a virgin when they married—a little frightened, a little embarrassed, but eager, because she'd waited a very long time for that special night. It had been disastrous. Aiden had made no attempt to be either tender or careful. He had been abrupt, rough and unconcerned with her feelings. She told herself it was because he was young, and that maybe it was her fault, because she had insisted they put off intimacy until they married. She'd been sure that once they became accustomed to each other, it would be different, better.

It did get a little better with time. Not great, never really satisfying, just better. But after Mustafa and his father had come and gone, everything changed. She became little more than an object for Aiden's release, and she'd hated it.

She had told herself after she left him that she'd had enough of intimacy to last her a lifetime, that if a man even tried to kiss her again, she'd head in the other direction as fast as her legs could carry her. But she hadn't run last night.

With her eyes still closed, she smiled.

And Brennan said, "Maybe it's time you hauled it out, Miss Jenny."

She opened her eyes and saw him standing over her.

"What time is it?" she asked, feeling her face flush because while he'd been watching her, she'd been thinking about him.

"Almost eight."

"You should have wakened me. We've got almost a day's walk and it's already hot."

"We're not walking." He pointed to a cloud of dust in the distance. "If I'm not mistaken, that's Gus Crocket heading our way."

Jenny sat up. "Gus? How did he know where to find us?"

"I told him that if we didn't come back in a couple of days, it meant you were tougher than I thought you were and that he was to come and get us in two weeks." He hunkered down on the sand, facing her. Reaching out, he brushed a strand of hair back from her face. "I know there've been times these last two weeks when you hated my guts, Jenny. But you didn't give up. You took everything I dished out. You didn't bitch or whine or cry uncle. I admire the hell out of you for that. Now I think you deserve a little R and R, so when Gus gets here I'm going to have him drive us over to Furnace Creek Inn.''

She beamed a hundred-watt smile and said, ''We're not walking? We're going someplace where I can have an honest-to-God bath?''

''And a steak and baked potatoes and maybe even a drink with ice in it.''

''It's too much,'' she said with a laugh. ''You're too good to me, Brennan.''

I'd like to be, he thought suddenly. I'd like to spoil you and pet you and and keep you smiling the way you're smiling now. Then, because he felt that unfamiliar edge of softness in himself, he said, ''Haul it out, Jenny. Gus'll be here in five minutes. It's time to break camp.''

She scrambled up, and when she saw the cloud of dust coming closer, began to help Mike pack what remained of their supplies.

Gus Crocket roared to a stop in front of the camp. ''By golly, you're right where you said you'd be,'' he called out when the Jeep rolled to a stop. He took his straw hat off, slapped it against the side of his overalls and shook hands with Mike.

''You-all doing all right?'' he asked. ''I been worried, 'specially about the little lady.'' He smiled at her and the creases around his sky-blue eyes deepened. ''You don't look none the worse for wear, ma'am. Still pretty as a desert sunrise. I gotta confess that I didn't think too highly of Mike, totin' you off way out here like he did. Kept telling myself he must've had a reason to make a little bit of a woman like you walk instead of ride.''

"Ride?" Jenny looked at Gus, then at Brennan. "Do you mean . . . are you trying to tell me you *chose* to have us hike all the way out here?"

"Well, yeah," Mike said with a grin. "I thought the walk would do you good."

"You—you . . . !" She was angry, so angry she was all but hopping up and down. She'd walked for two days through sun and sand, gotten blisters because of the damn boots he'd made her wear, carried a twenty-five pound pack and everything else he'd slung around her neck, and all the time they could have driven!

Hands on her hips, she glared up at him, but before she could say anything, he said, "Just think of it as part of the training, Miss Jenny. I wanted to see if you could hack it. I figured you'd give up after about two or three hours and we'd head back to the Junction."

He smiled and shook his head. "But you didn't give up. You took anything I had to dish out, and I'm proud of you."

"Well," she said. Her anger faded, and she felt inordinately pleased.

"So, like I said, you deserve a little R and R." He turned to Gus Crocket. "We're going over to the Furnace Creek Inn for a couple of days. Would you mind driving us over and coming back for us day after tomorrow?"

"Sure thing, Mike. I reckon Miss Jenny here would appreciate a couple of days of doing nothing." He scratched his head. "Don't know why you brung her out here in the first place."

Mike hesitated. Then, without looking at her, he said to Gus, "We're going into another desert country. I had to make sure she could hack it."

Jenny's heart leapt in a rush of emotion, of triumph and of joy. All that she had been through these last two weeks had been worth it. She'd convinced Mike Brennan that she was tough enough and strong enough to be in on the rescue of her son. She looked up at him and everything she was thinking showed in her eyes.

"You—you really are taking me with you," she said.

He squeezed her shoulder. "Yes, Miss Jenny, I surely am."

He hoped to hell he wasn't making a mistake.

It was a real hotel, with air-conditioning, a palm-shaded terrace and a swimming pool. As soon as Jenny entered her room, she shucked out of her clothes, drew a bath and with a contented sigh slipped into the warm soapy water. After two weeks of spit-and-polish baths, this was sheer heaven.

She soaked for a long time, and when she got out she looked at herself in the bathroom mirror. Her arms and legs were nut-brown, her face was tan, her hair, bleached by the sun, was two shades lighter. She looked in better shape than she'd been since she was twenty-one.

Her breasts were as firm and shapely as they had been then, her waist as small, her stomach as flat. Why hadn't Aiden valued her? Why had he taken her with so little love, so little caring? Why had he used her as though she were a chattel, something to satisfy his pleasure when he was in the mood, something to beat when he wasn't?

By the time their six-year marriage ended he had taken almost every bit of her self-confidence, her pride and her self-esteem.

These last two weeks in the desert had given her back her pride, and she was more thankful than she could ever say to Mike Brennan for giving her back this part of herself.

He was a strange man. He acted tough and talked tough, but she had a gut-deep feeling that he, unlike Aiden, had never raised his hand to strike a woman. The next few weeks would be dangerous, but she was unafraid, because Brennan would be with her. Together, please God, they would find Timmie and bring him back where he belonged.

After she rested, Jenny got up, dressed in her wrinkled shorts and a shirt, and went downstairs to the shop she'd noticed in the lobby. Mike had said they'd have dinner later, and she was darned if she wanted to look like a mule-skinning prospector.

She found a dark red Indian-style, ankle-length skirt, an off-the-shoulder white blouse and a white bathing suit. When the cashier was ringing up her purchases, Jenny saw a few bottles of perfume behind the counter. One was of a musky floral scent that she liked and she bought it. For too long she'd smelled of desert heat and desert sand; she wanted to smell like a woman again.

Brennan phoned her room at six. "How about a drink before dinner?" he asked. "I'll meet you out on the terrace."

"How soon?"

"Fifteen minutes?"

"Okay." She wasn't quite sure why she felt an unaccountable flush of pleasure. She'd just spent the toughest two weeks of her life with a man who, until last night, had treated her like a rookie he was determined to break. She should have had enough of him to last a lifetime, yet she could hardly wait to see him again. That was strange and more than a little disquieting.

She put on the blouse and skirt, brushed her hair loose about her shoulders, touched pale coral lipstick to her lips and a dab of perfume behind her ears.

"Not bad," she said when she looked at herself in the mirror. And grinned because she felt good and because in a couple of minutes she'd be with him again.

He was waiting for her under a pink-and-white-striped umbrella. He stood when he saw her and pulled out a chair. "You look..." He hesitated, nodded and said, "Not too bad for a desert rat."

"Gee, thanks." Jenny sat down and looked at his glass. "What're you having?"

"Gin and tonic. Sound good?"

"Sounds great."

He shoved a dish of peanuts toward her. "Did you rest?"

"For a little while."

"Actually, you look better than not too bad," he said. "You look terrific."

"Cut it out, Brennan. You'll have me thinking there's a soft streak somewhere under that tough exterior."

"God forbid!" He took a swallow of his drink and signaled for the waitress. When he'd ordered for Jenny, he said, "I know it's been a tough two weeks. How're you feeling?"

"Better than in a long time." She leaned toward him. "What's next?"

"We've got to get you a new passport and pictures and an entry visa. I've booked us on a commercial flight into Jahan. That's the easy part. But you need to know that it won't be that easy getting out. I want you to be aware that there's a risk, a great risk involved. If we're nabbed, your son will be sent back to his father and they'll probably lock me up for a couple of years." He looked her square in the eye. "But it won't go that easy for you, Jenny. There are no equal rights for women in Jahan."

He picked up his drink again and took another gulp. "A few years ago a woman was stoned to death there because she was suspected of being unfaithful to her husband. Last month a prostitute was hanged. From what you've said, the Huranis are an influential family. If we're caught, they'll charge you with kidnapping. I'm not sure what the penalty is for that." He leaned forward, his eyes serious, intent on hers. "I've promised to take you with me, and I still will, if you insist. But I wish you'd think about the danger involved."

"I've thought about it." Jenny waited until the waitress put her drink in front of her and left again before she said, "I'll do whatever you tell me to do, Mike. I'll follow orders and I won't complain. But I have to be a part of this. I don't think I'm particularly brave. The idea of being captured and at the mercy of someone like Aiden or his brother, Mustafa, terrifies me. But Timmie's my son. I have to go."

She was not like anyone he'd ever known. She touched him in a way he did not understand. He didn't want her to go to Jahan, not because she might hinder him, but because the thought of her being in danger scared the hell out of him.

In the glow of the desert sunset, her skin was a smooth and rosy tan. She was beautiful and scented and delectably feminine, the kind of a woman a man... He pulled himself up short. He never had and would not now mix business with pleasure. Jenny had been through a lot this last year or two. Her marriage had failed and her boy had been kidnapped. She was vulnerable, and a man, if he was any kind of a man, didn't take advantage of a vulnerable woman.

Get hold of yourself, he told himself. This is just another job and she's just another dame. Don't let your judgment get clouded by a pair of soft gray eyes and legs a man could die for.

"Look," Jenny said, breaking in on his thoughts. "Look how the sunset is changing the color of everything. The mountains are all purple shadows and the sand looks like gold. Isn't it beautiful, Mike? Isn't it just absolutely beautiful?"

"Beautiful," he said. But he wasn't looking at the sunset.

They had inch-thick steaks, mushrooms, green salads and fresh asparagus for dinner. And they talked as new friends do who had suddenly discovered they like each other.

"We'll take it easy tomorrow," Brennan told her over a final glass of red wine. "When Gus picks us up, we'll head to L.A. and take care of the passports and visas. We leave Sunday morning."

Sunday. By Monday she'd be in Jahan. She didn't know how long it would take to get to Timmie, but at least she'd be closer to him. It wouldn't be long now.

"I want to thank you," she said. "For everything you've done, for what you're doing."

"All in a day's work."

She smiled a little uncertainly, disappointed in a way she couldn't explain that it wasn't more than just a day's work to him. And told herself she was being foolish. This was business. She had hired him to do a job. They'd get Timmie out of Jahan and then it would be over. She and Brennan would shake hands, she'd go back to her life with her son, he'd go back to whatever dangerous job came next.

That depressed her, but she wasn't sure why.

A little after ten Brennan walked her to her room. "Sleep late in the morning and have your breakfast sent up." He rested a hand on her shoulder. "You've had a tough two weeks, Jenny, and you've come through them like a trooper. You deserve a rest."

She waited, remembering last night's kiss.

He squeezed her shoulder. "G'night," he said. "Sleep well."

She went inside her room and, without turning on the light, went to stand on her balcony. The air was soft with the scent of sagebrush. She leaned on the railing and looked out at the endless desert plains, wondering why she felt so alone. Maybe it was because for the past two weeks she'd lived twenty-four hours a day with a man. She'd slept close to him at night, had had all of her meals with him, had been bullied and harangued by him. He was always there, and now that he wasn't, she was lonely.

Below her a dim light shone on the water in the pool. There were very few guests in the hotel; no one was around. The water looked inviting.

She went back inside and closed the drapes. After she had undressed, she put on the new white bathing suit, slipped out of her room and went down the stairs to the pool. There she sat on the edge, dangling her legs in the almost-warm water.

She listened to the silence and thought that there had never been a night as beautiful as this one. She no longer felt lonely, but rather as if she were a part of the night and of the desert. The fading quarter moon shone brightly in the starlit sky and she was glad that she was here.

As silently as a whisper, she slipped into the pool and began to swim in slow, reaching strokes that barely rippled the water. It was velvet soft against her skin. She closed her eyes and turned so that she lay facedown, drifting on the ever-so-slight motion of the water, at one with the night and the universe. Then she rolled onto her back and began to swim again, her body free and relaxed.

She did not know how long she swam, but when she paused at one end of the pool to push her hair back, she saw Mike Brennan standing above her. He was barefoot. He wore khaki trousers, nothing else.

"Mike?" she said, but he didn't answer.

He'd seen her when she'd slipped into the water. Her slim figure had been shadowed by moonlight and he'd watched, scarcely breathing, when she floated facedown as though adrift somewhere between water and sky.

For two weeks he had slept next to her without touching her, but there hadn't been a moment when he hadn't been aware of her beside him. He had listened to her breathing, had watched the gentle rise and fall of her breasts, and he had ached to hold her.

He'd felt the same urge tonight when he'd walked her back to her room. It had taken every bit of his willpower not to sweep her into his arms. He longed to kiss her as he had last night at their desert camp. Longed to pick her up and carry her into her bed, to feel her body close to his, to make slow, deep love to her.

But he hadn't even touched her. He'd gone to his own room. He'd paced the floor, wanting a cigarette, wanting her. At last he'd gone out onto his balcony, and that's when he'd seen her below in the pool, her body slender and graceful as she slipped so silently into the water.

Now he stood above her. His heart was pounding, his mouth dry. He knew a longing he had never known before.

"How long have you been standing there?" she asked, looking up at him.

"Long enough."

The light that illuminated the pool dimmed and slowly faded to darkness. He held his hand down to her. "Come out," he said.

She hesitated for a fraction of a second before she reached out a hand to him. He pulled her up, and when he did, she said with a breathless laugh, "I'll get you all wet."

He didn't say anything. He only looked at her. Then he cupped her face between his hands and kissed her.

She was all silky softness in his arms. He ran his hands down her water-slick back to press her closer. He kissed her with hunger and with need, and whatever thoughts he'd had about keeping their relationship strictly professional faded in the warmth of her mouth. If she didn't step away from him . . .

She didn't step away. She molded her body to his and answered his kiss with a passion that set the blood racing through his veins. When he let her go, she looked up at him, and her eyes in the shadowed moonlight were lucent.

"Don't, Jenny," he murmured. "Don't look at me like that."

"Mike," she said. "Oh, Mike." She rested her head on his bare chest and felt the beat of his heart against her cheek.

He put a finger under her chin and lifted her face to his. "Something's happening here," he said.

"I know."

"Turn and walk away before it's too late, Jenny."

She took a shuddering breath, and the corners of her mouth curved in a trembling smile. "But I'm afraid of the dark," she said. "I don't want to be alone."

He took her hand and brought it to his lips. Then he turned it and she felt the heat of his tongue against her palm. She closed her eyes, and when she opened them, he put his arm around her. They went into the hotel and climbed the stairs. When they passed her room, she didn't say anything.

They went on down the hall. He opened the door of his room, and hesitated. Then he took her hand and led her in.

For a little while they didn't speak. He put his arms around her and she said, "I think I'm a little afraid of this."

He kissed the side of her face. "Don't be," he said. "It's going to be all right."

He kissed her mouth and gentled her with his hands. She felt very small and fragile. He thought of the man who had abused her and was overwhelmed with a feeling of tenderness.

"It's cool in here," he said. "You need to get out of that wet suit." And because he sensed her shyness, he took his shirt off the back of the chair and handed it to her.

She went into the bathroom to take the suit off and put his shirt on. It came to the middle of her thighs. She dried her hair as best she could with a towel, and quickly, before she could change her mind, went out to him.

He drew her into his arms, and again, as he had out by the pool, he kissed her with hunger and with need. When her lips parted, he slipped his arms around her waist and brought her closer. His hands slid up and he pushed the shirt aside so that he could caress her breasts. She shivered, and when she made as though to draw away, he said, "Let me touch you like this. Please, Jenny."

She felt so many conflicting emotions—excitement, heat, fear of the unknown. The kiss deepened. Her body softened and she responded, responded until sudden vivid flashes of memory came unbidden into her mind. The memory of having been partially aroused, only to be left suspended, unsatisfied. Other memories of hurt and pain, of being taken before she was ready. Of a hand slashing across her face because she had cried out and tried to move away. Of bruises on her breasts, and on her wrists where he had pinned her down.

She started to tremble.

"What is it?" Mike asked. "Jenny, what is it?"

She shook her head and clung to him. He kissed her and the bad memories faded.

When the trembling stopped, he picked her up and carried her to his bed. He laid her down and took his trousers off. She turned away, afraid again. But when he came in beside her and took her into his arms, his mouth was gentle against hers. He kissed her for a long time. He soothed a hand over her shoulders and her back, then began to caress her breasts. And finally, when her body was soft and pliant against his, he eased himself over her.

"It will be good, Jenny," he whispered against her throat. "I promise you, it will be good." Gently, carefully, he joined his body to hers. And kissed her, content to wait until she accommodated herself to him before he moved more deeply.

It was... okay. He hadn't hurt her. His body was warm and strong. This was... all right. It was comforting to be close to him this way. It was... hmm... actually it was a lot more than all right. It was nice. Very nice.

He kissed her again, deeply, urgently, and murmured his pleasure when he touched his tongue to hers. He leaned to kiss her breast, to lap and tease a nipple.

It became more than nice. Quite indescribable. Something was definitely happening here. Something she'd never before experienced.

"Sweetheart," he whispered against her lips as he began to move faster, deeper. "Ah, Jenny. Little Jenny."

She clung to him and tightened her hands on his shoulders. "Mike?" she whispered, not sure this was really happening to her. "Oh, Mike. This is so... so good."

"The way I knew it would be," he whispered against her lips.

He rocked her closer, so close that she became a part of him. He moved with frantic urgency against her, all the while murmuring his delight against her lips, stroking her, touching her breasts, bringing her to a peak of ecstasy she'd never known.

"Oh!" she said. "Oh, I—I..."

There were no words, only an unbelievably wonderful, senses-reeling feeling. She spun out of focus, lifting her body to his, whimpering with a pleasure so keen it was almost past bearing.

He thrust deep and his body shook hard against hers. He took her mouth, he took her cry, and they moved together, helpless in the grip of their passion.

He collapsed over her, his face against her throat. "Jenny," he whispered over and over again. "Oh, Jenny."

She clung to him. She stroked his hair, kissed his shoulder. And felt hot tears sting her eyes because she hadn't known, hadn't even guessed that making love could be like this.

He raised himself over her and looked into her eyes. He kissed her. "It was so good," he murmured. "So right."

She touched the side of his face, and in a voice so soft he could barely hear, she whispered, "This—this was the first time. I mean I've never—never ... You know."

His body stilled. "Never?" he asked with awe in his voice.

She shook her head.

"Oh, Jenny," he said. "Jenny." He kissed her eyes, her nose, her cheeks, and lips still swollen from his kisses. He held her close and told her how fine she was, how dear.

And his heart was near to bursting, because with him she had experienced something she never had with the man who had been her husband.

She nestled against him, her head against his chest, and he sensed that she was shy now that she'd told him. He kissed the top of her head and tightened his arms around her. He whispered her name in the quiet of the night, and the sound of it was like a prayer upon his lips.

Chapter 5

She was somewhere in that quiet place between sleeping and waking, her body warm against his, her head on his shoulder. With her awakening came the memory of the night before, a shadowy dream moving into conscious thought.

Mike Brennan had made love to her. No, that wasn't right, he had made love *with* her. There was a difference. She hadn't merely been a means for his satisfaction; they had shared the experience of lovemaking.

She hadn't known it could be like that and now, strangely, the sense of regret of all that she had missed during her six years of marriage to Aiden was mixed with the joy of discovery. Michael Bernard Brennan, who came off as being so overpoweringly macho tough, had taken her to heights she had never dreamed possible. And afterward, unlike Aiden, who had always turned away once he had satisfied himself, Mike had held and petted her, whispering tender words until she slept.

Her friends in college had talked about earth-shaking, mind-boggling sex. She had listened, laughed when they'd laughed and made no comment. Later, after she and Aiden had been married for a few months, she'd had lunch with the same group.

"Well?" Rosa Hernandez had asked. "How's it going?"

"Fine," Jenny had said. "Wonderful."

Rosa grinned at her. "Aiden's a handsome dude, Jen. Dark, mysterious, Arabian. I knew the first time I saw him he'd be a sensational lover. And he is, right?"

"Of course." She'd looked down at her spinach soufflé. "Of course," she'd repeated. Then she'd looked up and seen Josie McCall looking at her, compassion in her nice green eyes.

When Jenny had told Josie she was going to marry Aiden, Josie had raised an eyebrow. "You don't know anything about him," she'd said. "Arab men are different—I don't think I like them. I don't like Aiden. There's something about him..." She'd hesitated. "Don't do it, Jen," she said. "Wait a while. Don't rush into this."

Jenny hadn't listened. She'd married Aiden, and she had never admitted to either one of her best friends what a terrible mistake she had made, or that she had never truly experienced fulfillment.

She hadn't known until last night how really wonderful making love could be. Now, needing to touch Mike, to reassure herself it had really happened for her, she turned her head and kissed his shoulder.

"Umm," he murmured.

"I'm sorry. I didn't mean to wake you."

"'S all right. Nice way to wake up." He gathered her in his arms and nuzzled his chin against the spill of her hair. "Sleep okay?"

"Fine." She rose on her elbow and looked down at him. His thick black hair was rumpled; his eyes were the same color blue as the Pacific on a sunny day. "It's late," she said. "I suppose we should get up."

"Why?"

"You're not hungry?"

"Yeah, I'm hungry, but not for bacon and eggs." He reached out and eased her over so that she lay on top of him. "Last night was pretty special," he said. "It made me hungry for more."

"Oh?" She smiled, then blushed and dropped her head against his shoulder.

"Don't be sorry that we made love," he said.

"I'm not."

He stroked her hair, remembering how it had been. The sensible part of him knew that making love to Jenny hadn't been such a good idea. When they went into Jahan, he'd have to think like a pro and behave like a pro. That would be hard to do if they were emotionally involved, if he let his concern for her safety get in the way of the job.

But the other part of him felt like rejoicing, because making love with Jenny had been the nicest thing that had ever happened to him. It excited the hell out of him that he had pleased her, that because of him she had experienced something she had not felt in her years of marriage to Hurani. It made him want to beat on his chest and roar like a lion. It also humbled him and made him feel something he'd never felt before. That scared the bejesus out of him.

The bad thing—or the good thing, depending on how you looked at it—was that last night had only whetted his appetite for more.

He laced his fingers through her hair to bring her closer. "Jenny," he whispered against her lips. His body hardened with need and it became as it had last night.

She'd been pretty sure that all of the mysterious and wonderful new sensations she'd felt with him had been a once-in-a-lifetime thrill, a fluke, a never-again-to-be-experienced miracle of pleasure, because surely nothing could be that good twice. But as they began to make love again, it became as good—no, even better—than it had been last night.

He kissed her as though he could not get enough of her lips. He sampled, he tasted, he touched his tongue to hers. He caressed her breasts as though they were the most precious, the most perfect breasts in the world. He stroked her back. He told her how pretty she was, how soft, how much he liked to touch her.

Her body melted with pleasure, but with the pleasure came the scary feeling that if she didn't hurry, he might become impatient. The way Aiden always had. In the early days of their marriage she had sometimes reached this plateau, only to be left suspended because Aiden had not had the patience to wait or to try to please her.

Mike was a tough and impatient man, obviously an experienced man as far as women were concerned. He'd been nice last night because it had been their first time, but probably now he'd expect her to be more skilled, more . . . ready.

And because she was afraid this moment would pass, that he *would* get impatient, she moved so that

she was beneath him, so that he could take her now if
that was what he wanted. Take her before the excitement she was beginning to feel passed.

"In a minute, Jenny," he murmured. "Let me sa-
vor you." He kissed her again, slowly, deeply. Kissed
her until she was breathless and yearning. Until her
skin burned and every nerve ending tingled with excitement.

She entwined her arms around his neck, holding
him because she didn't want the kissing to stop. But
when he left her mouth to take her breasts, to suckle
and tease her yearning nipples, she whispered, "Oh,
yes," and held him there.

Love play. It was something she'd never known before. His whispered sighs of enjoyment told her that
this was as good for him as it was for her, that they
didn't have to hurry, that they could pleasure each
other like this until the sensations became unbear-
able.

He kissed her belly and her hips. He made soft love
bites on the inside of her thighs, and sprinkled delicious kisses across her skin. He brushed his lips across
the apex of her legs and gently caressed her there.

So good. So much. Waves of heat suffused her
body, and when she began to tremble with a need too
long held in check, he brought her closer. She felt him
hard against her leg, and knew again, as she had last
night, that brief moment of fear—and of regret, because she didn't want this to end.

And perhaps he sensed it, because he came up to
cradle her in his arms, to kiss her mouth and to whisper how good this was for both of them, how much he
loved to touch her and hold her. Only when she relaxed again did he join his body to hers.

It was as she remembered. He moved against her, strong and sure, fierce but gentle, and when she lifted her body to his, the strokes became faster, deeper. He plunged and withdrew, to plunge again. And each time he did, she cried out, "Oh, yes. Oh, yes."

He encircled her back to bring her closer, and rocked her to an ecstasy unlike anything she had ever known. He kissed her. He touched her breasts with tender fingers, gently squeezing a nipple, lightly scraping a fingernail across the rigid peak. And when her body began to quiver beneath his, he whispered, "Yes, Jenny? Now, Jenny?"

But she was beyond words. She could only cling to him and let this immensity of feeling wash over her. It shook her to her very roots as she lifted her body to his in an agony of release.

He covered her mouth with his and gripped her as if he would never let her go when his body convulsed in a fever of passion against hers.

Later, as he held her and stroked her to calmness, Mike told himself that no matter how good this was between them, it was wrong. It shouldn't happen again. He wouldn't let it happen again. He wouldn't...

But even as the thought came, he knew that he lied.

Jenny wasn't happy about having her hair cut, but the woman who fitted her for the black wig said, "If you're going to wear this for a long period of time, it's better to have your hair short. It'll be more comfortable for you and we'll get a better fit."

And so her hair was cut, no more than an inch long all over her head. She looked, she thought, like a curly haired boy. But the change was even worse when she had the wig on. It was black, with a side part, and came to just about an inch below her ear.

The woman, someone a connection of Brennan's had recommended, studied Jenny's face. "Now we'll see what we can find in glasses for you."

She poked around in a worktable drawer and took out several pairs—one heavy, black and horn-rimmed; one tortoiseshell; a pair of round frames that Jenny thought would make her look like an owl.

The woman picked up the round ones. "These might do," she said.

But Jenny shook her head and reached for the tortoiseshell ones. The glass was clear. The frames weren't great, but they were better than either the horn-rimmed or the owly ones.

Next came the application of a darker shade of makeup than Jenny usually used, and a darker lipstick that was extended over her lipline. When that was done the woman handed her the glasses. Jenny put them on, then turned to the mirror. She looked different, older.

"Voilà!" the other woman said, obviously pleased. "You are very different, yes?"

"Yes, very."

The woman glanced at her watch, then handed Jenny a slip of paper. "You are to meet Mr. Brennan at this address at one-thirty. It's now a little after one. You'll be able to get a cab in front of the building."

"Do I pay you?" Jenny asked.

"No, it's been taken care of. You'd better go. The man who will take care of your passport doesn't like to be kept waiting."

Jenny went out into the hall toward the elevator. When she passed a mirror, she came to a dead stop and stared at her reflection. A foreign-looking woman, older, not very attractive, gazed back at her.

The elevator came. It was crowded when she got on and she felt as though everybody in it was staring at her. It was the same when she went out onto the street and got into a taxi. But when she gave the driver the address off Sepulveda, he paid no attention to her.

The two-story building he stopped in front of was shabby and rundown. The sign above the door read J. Goodwin & Sons, Printers. She went in. Five or six people were waiting in a small reception room. They looked up when she entered, then back down at the magazines they were reading. She took a chair next to the receptionist's desk, and because she was unsure whether or not to give her name, said nothing.

A few minutes later the door to one of the inside offices opened. Brennan came out. He looked around at the people who were waiting, glanced at his watch, frowned and started to go back inside.

Jenny stood. "Uh, hi," she said.

His eyes went wide. He stared at her for a moment or two before he said, "In here," and held the door open for her to enter.

A middle-aged man with a sparsity of hair and an unruly, frizzled beard that came halfway down his chest motioned her inside. He took in the trim, navy blue suit and the frilly blouse she was wearing and shook his head. "Won't do," he told Brennan.

He looked through the rack of clothes at one end of the room, found a black blouse with a high neck and long sleeves and handed it to Jenny. "There's a dressing room right through there," he said. "Put this on while I get the camera ready."

She did as she was told, but she didn't like it. The blouse, besides being unattractive, was too big. When she went out into the other room, the man—Mike called him Goodwin—nodded and said, "Yep. That's better."

Than what? she wondered. She glanced at Mike. He grinned and shrugged.

"Have a seat, Mrs. O'Brien." Goodwin gestured to the chair in front of the camera.

Mrs. O'Brien. That gave her pause. Nervously she adjusted the glasses and sat down.

Goodwin told her which way to look and snapped the picture. "Passports'll be ready tomorrow at ten," he told Mike. "Five hundred bucks, payable now."

Mike counted out the bills.

"Can I take the wig and the glasses off?" Jenny asked.

Brennan's grin deepened. "I'd appreciate it if you would, Mrs. B."

Mrs. B. Her stomach fluttered and she went into the other room to change.

When they left Goodwin's, they went shopping for Jenny's new wardrobe: dark, conservative clothes, dresses that were a size too big, skirts, long-sleeved blouses, a too-big black jacket. And more desert clothes—pants and shirts and sturdy shoes. Just in case.

She thought about the sixteen thousand she'd given Mike and wondered how long it would last.

On Saturday night she telephoned her folks. Her mother cried and her father said, "You're sure you want to do this?"

"Yes, Dad," she answered. "It's something I have to do."

"Then our prayers go with you, Geneva. God bless you and keep you safe."

Her mother, still sniffing but trying to hold back her tears, came on the line. "Princess Pat will be foaling in another few weeks," she said. "You tell Timmie as soon as you see him that his granddad says the foal is his."

"I will, Mama."

"I love you, Geneva."

"I love you, too. Both you and Daddy."

She sighed when she put the phone down, and Brennan, who had been standing in the open door connecting their two rooms, said, "Tough call?"

Jenny nodded. "My mother's pretty upset. My dad's going to give Timmie the new foal when it comes."

He came into the room. "The boy will like that."

"Yes." She looked up at him, her gray eyes anxious, appealing. "We're going to do it, aren't we, Mike? We're going to find Tim and bring him back, aren't we?"

He rested his hand on her head. "Yes," he said. And prayed that it was true.

The flight left at ten on Sunday morning. Mr. and Mrs. Michael O'Brien were assigned seats in the business-class section. Mr. O'Brien read the sports section of the L.A. *Times* during takeoff; Mrs. O'Brien clutched the armrests and prayed the plane wouldn't crash.

When he realized what she was doing, Mike said, surprised, "You don't like to fly?"

"I'm pretty good once we're up." She tried to smile. "But takeoffs and landings scare me to death."

"It's safer than driving the L.A. freeways."

"Maybe."

He put the paper down and squeezed her hand. "It's going to be a long flight," he said. "Why don't you try to rest?"

"Rest?" She shook her head. "I'm too busy listening to the motors." She tightened her hand around his. "How long before we get to Jahan?"

"Six hours to New York, Jenny. Another six to Paris. We'll overnight there and fly to Jahan tomorrow."

Tomorrow. Jenny lay back in her seat and closed her eyes. She knew that what she was doing was risky, but she would have taken any risk, no matter what the cost, to get her son back where he belonged.

For as long as she lived, she would remember that terrible moment when she'd realized that Aiden had kidnapped Timmie. The court, beside allowing visitation rights, had given Aiden permission to take Timmie one weekend a month. Every time that happened she had been afraid.

On that Saturday morning six months ago, her fear had turned into unreasoning panic. Timmie had been dressed and ready when his father arrived. He'd clung to her and whispered, "I don't want to go, Mama. I want to stay with you and Grandma and Grandpa."

She'd hugged him and, because she didn't want to upset him, said, "You'll have a fine time with your dad, Tim. And when he brings you back tomorrow, we'll have a welcome-home party with hamburgers and french fries and chocolate ice cream. Okay?"

"'Kay," he'd said. But he'd tightened his arms around her neck and she'd known he hadn't wanted to go.

Aiden had taken Timmie's hand and led him to the car.

"Bye-bye," she'd called from the front porch. Then suddenly, feeling as though her heart were being torn from her body, she'd cried, "Wait!" and had run down the steps to the car.

"One more hug," she'd said. She kissed him. "I love you, baby. I love you so much." And to Aiden she'd said, "Remember, you're to have him back by four tomorrow afternoon."

"Of course." And he'd smiled, the way he did sometimes just before he hit her.

Aiden hadn't come at four the next day. At five she'd called the house in San Diego. A recorded message had come on and an impersonal voice said, "That number is no longer in service."

She called the police. They said, "If your boy's not back by morning, give us a call."

She had no intention of waiting until morning. She and her father drove to the house in San Diego she and Aiden had shared for the six years of their marriage. She was out of the car before it had come to a full stop, running up the front steps, pounding on the door. There hadn't been any answer. She still had her key, but she was shaking so badly, her father had to take it away from her and open the door.

She'd rushed in. The living room was bare. On legs that threatened to give way, she'd run into Aiden's room. It, too, was empty and his clothes were gone. She'd slumped against a wall, sliding down before her father could reach her.

They'd gone to a next-door neighbor. "Mr. Hurani sold everything last week," the woman said. "Saturday morning he put some suitcases in the trunk of his car. He told me and my husband he was going away for good."

Her father drove her to the police station. She'd been almost too numb with fear to speak.

"We'll do what we can," the police said, "but very likely, from what you've told us, your husband has already taken the boy out of the country."

The days that followed passed in a blur of emotional pain unlike anything Jenny had ever know. The police couldn't do anything. The State Department confirmed that Mr. Hurani had obtained a passport for his son. They told her there was nothing they could do. Then her congressman had answered her letter saying that he was sorry but he could not help her.

That's when she had gone to Command, Inc. and found Mike Brennan.

Jenny opened her eyes and studied his face. She had only known him for a little less than three weeks, yet she was trusting him with her life and with her son's safety. She looked at his hands. The fingers were long and blunt, the nails clipped and clean. The palm of his right hand was callused, the knuckles thick. Tough hands, a man's hands.

She knew so little about him. She surmised that he had been in many battles, that he had wounded and been wounded. The life he led was a dangerous one, and she thought that very likely he did the work he did because he liked the danger as much, perhaps even more than, the money.

When lunch was served she only picked at it. She tried to read a magazine, but her eyes wouldn't focus. All she could think about was this trip, and that every mile brought her closer to her son. She wanted to make the plane go faster so that she could get to him. Timmie. Timmie.

She took a small envelope of pictures of herself with Timmie out of her purse and looked at them. She'd brought them along to show him in case he was frightened, in case he didn't remember her. Six months was a long time when you were four and a half. Would he remember her?

She'd brought his favorite toy, too—Jerry, the orange giraffe. Surely he'd remember Jerry.

She put the photographs back in her purse, and at last, exhausted, went to sleep.

When they reached New York they transferred to the international terminal, where they waited two hours for their Paris flight to leave. She wanted to take the wig and the glasses off, but Brennan wouldn't let her.

"This is your persona now, so you'd better get used to it."

"We're in New York," she said. "Nobody here knows who we are or that we're going to Jahan."

But he wouldn't budge. They were going on a dangerous mission. There were foreign agents, as well as agents of his own government, who kept their eyes on him. It was entirely possible that Aiden Hurani had Jahanian friends in the U.S. watching Jenny. Mike didn't think they'd been followed, but he wasn't taking any chances. In case they were, the black wig and glasses Jenny wore would help.

He knew how nervous she was. She hadn't slept well last night, and though she had tried not to awaken him, he had been aware of her restlessness. "What is it?" he'd asked. "Can't you sleep?"

"I keep thinking about tomorrow," she'd said.

He'd put his arms around her. "Tomorrow night we'll be in Paris. We'll have diner in a restaurant I know on the Champs Élysées and afterward we'll walk along the Seine and neck, just like the Parisians."

She'd tried to smile, and when she couldn't, said, "I'm scared, Mike. Not for me—for my safety, I mean—but scared that we won't be able to pull it off. If we fail—"

"We're not going to fail." He tightened his arms around her. "We're going to find your son," he said. "We're going to bring him home."

He looked at her now, her eyes closed, her face turned toward him. She was twenty-nine, almost eleven years younger than he was. The wig and the dark clothes made her look older, but even with the disguise, she was still a beautiful woman.

He wished he'd left her behind, wished he hadn't agreed to take her with him to Jahan. He reached over and put an arm around her so that he could bring her closer. She sighed and nestled against his shoulder. Jenny, he thought. Jenny.

He wakened her just before they reached Paris. She sat up and rubbed her eyes.

"Are we almost there?" she asked.

"Almost." He took her hand when the plane circled low over the city, and held it tight when they came in for a landing.

They took a taxi to the hotel where he'd made reservations. Jenny had never been abroad, and though she tried to enjoy the sights and sounds of Paris, she could not.

The hotel was modest but charming. From their window they could see the Eiffel Tower. The restaurant they went to was lovely, the food delicious, the wine full-bodied. And though afterward they walked along the Seine, where lovers young and old stopped in the shadows to kiss, they did not. It was as though, at least for now, everything except her desire to get to Timmie was on hold.

When they returned to the hotel on the Left Bank, she said, "I'm really tired, Mike," and went to sit on the edge of one of the twin beds.

"Then get some sleep, Jen. Tomorrow's going to be a long day."

He kissed her and got into the other bed. Long after he heard her steady breathing and knew that at last she slept, he lay looking up at the ceiling. By tomorrow night they would be in Jahan. It was a dangerous and primitive country. He would do his damnedest to get her kid out, but if it came to a choice between Jenny's safety and getting her son back to the States, he'd have no choice—he'd think of Jenny first. Because he cared about her. A hell of a lot more than he wanted to.

Chapter 6

For over an hour there had been nothing to see except endless miles of sand below, slanting dunes and dust-dry mountains that rose eerily in the vast, uninhabited wilderness.

This was Aiden's land. It was where he had come from, where he had taken their child. As the plane began to circle lower, Jenny could see a few villages dotted against the landscape. Timmie was somewhere down there, her little boy, lost in this strange and foreign land.

"We are approaching the city of Zagora," the attendant said, first in Jahanian, then in French, Spanish and English. "Please fasten your seat belts, ladies and gentlemen."

Jenny put her glasses on. "Do I look all right?" she asked nervously.

Mike took her hand. "You look fine," he said. "Your own mother wouldn't recognize you."

But will my son? she wondered. Will Timmie remember me? Will he remember how much I love him?

The plane came in low, touched the tarmac, bounced, and finally landed, braking hard. Jenny clasped Mike's hand and didn't let go until they'd rolled to a stop.

"We'll go through Immigration first, then Customs," he told her when he reached above their seats for the carry-on bag.

He tried to speak casually, as though coming to Jahan was an everyday occurrence. Their passports, though phony, were in order. They had their visas. It was going to be a cinch. That's what he told himself, but his stomach was in knots and his jaw was tight. If the authorities found out who Jenny was, that she'd come to take her son out of the country, he doubted either one of them would escape with their lives. For though he'd told her that capture would mean prison for him, he'd known when he'd taken her case the kind of danger he'd be walking into. They were in a life-and-death situation here. They had to be careful every step of the way.

When they stepped out the door of the plane, they were greeted by a blast of furnace-hot air, and men with rifles who shouted orders at them. The uniformed men waited until all of the passengers had deplaned, then formed a circle around them and, herding them together, motioned them toward the terminal.

Jenny's mouth was dry and there was a film of perspiration on her upper lip. Her scalp felt as if it was on fire and she longed to reach up under the wig and scratch.

The inside of the terminal was hot, airless. They were motioned to a line. Mike spoke to the man in

front of them, an Englishman here to do business with
an oil company. Yes, Immigration was a pain, the man
said. But it was the same in every country, wasn't it?
He looked as uneasy as Mike felt, but they both pretended this was just a normal procedure.

Suddenly, ahead of them, there was a commotion.
A man was yanked out of the line. When he protested, one of the uniformed men lowered his rifle and
two other men grabbed his arms. He shouted something and one of the officers slammed the barrel of his
rifle into the man's stomach. He doubled over and
they dragged him away.

There was a momentary buzz of voices before the
room grew silent. The passengers looked at each other
uneasily before their glances slid away and they stared
straight ahead.

Twenty minutes went by as the line crept forward.
Thirty. The man ahead of Brennan stepped over the
red line and presented his documents to the Immigration official. Brennan saw the beads of sweat on his
forehead. Questions were asked, answers mumbled.
The documents were stamped and the man hurried
toward the door marked Customs.

They were next. Mike took Jenny's arm and presented their passports. The official studied them, grim-
faced, stern. "Purpose of your trip?" he barked.

"To visit a friend," Mike said.

"How long will you stay?"

"Two or three weeks. I want to get in some hunting
while I'm here."

The stern gaze swung to Jenny. "This is your wife?"
he asked.

"Yes."

"If you are here to go hunting, why did you bring her along?"

Brennan grinned. "Because she wouldn't stay home. She insisted on coming with me."

"American men!" the official said with a snort of disgust. "You will never learn how to handle your women. Perhaps while you are here in Jahan you will take a few lessons from us."

"Maybe I will," Brennan said with a laugh.

The man stamped the passports. "All right," he said. "You can go. But remember that this is not the United States. Your wife cannot conduct herself here as she would in her own country. It would not be wise to let her go out alone."

Mike tightened his hand on her arm. "I have no intention of letting her out alone." He picked up the carry-on bag and they headed for Customs.

Their suitcases were stacked on the floor along with all the other passengers' luggage. Mike picked them up and carried them toward a Customs officer.

"Open!" the man commanded.

Mike opened the cases and put them up on the rack.

"The lady's purse."

Jenny tightened her hands around it. The envelope of photographs of herself with Timmie was in the bag. If the inspector saw it, saw her with blond hair, with Timmie... Panic gripped her. Why had she brought it? And the orange giraffe? They'd want to know why a grown woman was carrying a child's toy. Dear God, everything could end right here. What should she do?

Eyes wide with fear, she clutched the bag and looked at Brennan.

"The purse." The Customs man snapped his fingers impatiently.

"I—I..."

"Mike! Mike!"

Mike swung around and saw Kumar Ben Ari waving from the other side of the room. He pushed his way through the lines of passengers and Customs officials and strode toward them. He was taller than most of the men in the room, dark skinned and dark eyed, handsome in tailored pants, fine leather boots, a black silk shirt and black Arab head-covering.

"Marhaban!" he shouted. "Welcome! Welcome!" He reached out for Mike, brought him into the typical Arab embrace and kissed him on both cheeks before he turned to Jenny. "This is your wife, yes?" He bowed. "Welcome to Jahan. I hope we will make your stay a pleasant one." He turned to the Customs official. "Is there a problem?" he asked with a frown.

"No, *sidi.* I was about to examine the luggage. In this moment I asked to see the lady's purse."

"But why? That is a very personal item, is it not?"

"Yes, but—"

"Mr. and Mrs. O'Brien are friends of mine and I can vouch for them. Is that not enough? Do you question my word?"

"No, *sidi.* Of course not, *sidi.* Everything is in order." He closed their suitcases. "Your friends may go."

"Shukran, thank you." Kumar clapped a shoulder on Mike's arm. "Let us go then, my friend," he said. "Your woman can bring the bags."

Jenny looked up at him, unbelieving, but he and Mike had already turned and started toward the door. Fuming and muttering under her breath, adrenaline surging with her rising anger, she picked up the two suitcases and struggled after them. This was Brennan's good friend? This Arabian male chauvinist?

Someone opened the door. Kumar snapped his fingers and a black-robed chauffeur hurried forward to take the bags from her and put them in an expensive imported car. Then Kumar stood aside to let her enter.

She sat, arms across her chest, looking straight ahead, mad as a wet hen.

The two men got in. "I apologize for my bad manners," Kumar said. "I thought it best to behave like a Jahanian in front of the authorities. I almost had to break Mike's arm to make him come along with me. Please let me assure you that henceforth you will be treated like the lady you are."

"Some country!" She glared at him, then at Mike.

"I'm sorry, Jenny." Mike squeezed her hand. "We'll try not to let that happen again."

"Damn straight!" she said.

They pulled out of the airport and entered a boulevard lined with tall royal palms. Beyond the palms there was only sand for as far as Jenny could see. The sky was a cloudless blue, the air hot and crackling dry.

Mike and Kumar talked like old friends, but only about casual things. Now and then Kumar stole a look at Jenny, and once or twice he asked her how she had enjoyed the trip.

"I'm not a happy flier," she said. And anxious to learn how he was going to help them find Timmie, she started to ask, "Have you been able to learn anything about—"

"We're entering the city now," he said, cutting her off. "The building there is where the Jahanian Oil Company has its offices. The white building on your left is the National Bank of Jahan. The hotel is the Royal Jahanian.''

She looked at him, then at the chauffeur, and realized she'd almost done something stupid. In the same polite tone that he had used, she asked, "Is that where we'll be staying?''

"No, indeed, Mrs. O'Brien. You and Mike will be my guests for as long as you're in Jahan. While Mike and I are . . ." He shot Brennan a grin. "While we are hunting, you can relax and enjoy my house. There is a pool, of course, and a library filled with books in English. I'm sure you won't be bored while we're away.''

"I won't be bored," Jenny said with a tight little smile. "I intend to go hunting with you and Mike.''

"You want to go with us?" His dark eyes widened with disbelief. He looked at Mike and shook his head. "Impossible," he declared. "Quite impossible.''

"Nothing is impossible, Mr. Ben Ari.''

He shot her a frown that very likely had put the fear of both God and Allah into the hearts of other women. "This is Jahan, *madame*," he said. "We are a desert country—''

"I'm quite used to the desert," she said, breaking in before he could say anything else. "And I'm a good shot." She turned to Mike. "Tell him," she said.

"Yes," Brennan acknowledged. "You're a good shot, Jenny. But that doesn't mean you're going with us, because you're not.''

She gave him a look angry enough to melt his back teeth, then turned away and stared out of the window at the city of Zagora. To all outward appearances it was a busy, modern city. There were a lot of automobiles on the streets, most of them late-model luxury cars. The office buildings looked clean and white. A mosque rose higher than the other buildings, its bright mosaic patterns glinting in the afternoon sun.

"The seaport is to the north of here," Kumar said. "Near the town of D'anfa. The mountains, where Mike and I will hunt, are to the west."

West, where Timmie was. Jenny turned in the direction he had pointed and lowered the glasses on her nose, straining to see beyond the city, beyond the desert sands, out to the mountains where, somewhere in a village, she would find her son. No one, not Brennan or Kumar or Allah himself, would keep her from going to him.

Mama's coming Timmie, she whispered in her mind. Mama's coming.

Ten miles from the city they turned off the highway onto a private, palm-lined road. After they had gone perhaps a mile, Jenny saw a high stone wall. Two armed guards wearing purple uniforms stood on either side of an iron gate.

The car slowed to a stop. The guards snapped to attention and the gate was opened onto terraced lawns, fountains and flower gardens. Beyond lay a classically pure, stark white building with Moorish domes, arches, spires and turrets that glinted in the afternoon sun. Unbelievably beautiful, it looked, Jenny thought, like a castle straight out of the *Arabian Nights*.

"Be it ever so humble," Mike said with a grin. "It's good to be back, my friend."

"My home is your home." Kumar looked at Jenny. "Yours and your wife's, of course."

As soon as the car stopped, two servants dressed in white djellabas appeared and hurried forward to take the luggage out of the trunk.

"My humble home," Kumar said with a bow. "Please, come in."

A manservant opened a fifteen-foot-tall, gold-embossed door and they entered into a patio. Water bubbled from a center fountain. Orange and lemon trees heavy with fruit lined the sides of the patio, and there were flowers everywhere.

Kumar clapped his hands twice and a woman appeared. "This is Latife," he said to Jenny. "She will be your personal servant while you're here, Mrs. O'Brien. Go with her now and she will show you to your quarters."

Quarters? Jenny looked at Mike uncertainly.

"Go along," he said. "I'll see you later."

"We dine at eight," Kumar said. "Latife will bring you to us."

This was all very strange and foreign. She didn't want to leave Mike, but it appeared she didn't have a choice, and so she followed the woman down a marble corridor that led from one patio to another. Everything was pristine and white. The air was scented from the orange blossoms that floated on the waters in the sparkling fountains.

At last they passed though mosaic-encrusted Moorish arches that led to still another corridor. When they came to a brass-studded door, Latife paused and said, "Your rooms, *madame.*"

Everything in the first room was in a pale shade of blue. Pale gossamer curtains flowed from the floor-to-ceiling windows. The sofa and love seat were in a deeper shade of watered silk. There was a chaise, beautifully carved mahogany tables, gilt mirrors, flowering plants, a vase filled with white roses. And French doors that opened onto a patio.

The bedroom was as beautiful as the sitting room, but here everything was in shades of pale ivory.

"Perhaps you would like to bathe while I unpack, *madame,*" Latife said. "Then you will rest and I will come for you when it is time for dinner. If there is anything you desire, you have only to pick up the telephone and ask. Almost all of the servants speak English, so you will have no problem with the language."

"Very well," Jenny said. "Thank you, Latife."

"I will run your bath, *madame,*" the servant said, and went into the bathroom.

When she was alone, Jenny looked around. This kind of luxury would take some getting used to. But she had no intention of being here long enough to get used to it. She was in Jahan to find her son, and find him she would. If Mike Brennan and that chauvinist friend of his thought they were going to leave her behind, they had another think coming.

She took the glasses off, then the hated black wig, and ran her fingers through the short blond curls. When Latife came out of the bathroom, she looked at Jenny, too startled for a moment to speak. "Your— your bath is ready, *madame,*" she finally managed to say. Then, her dark eyes wide with amazement, she hurried out of the room.

The water in the black marble tub was scented with the perfume of roses. Rose petals floated on the surface. Jenny lay back and groaned with pleasure. Was this how the ladies in the days of sheiks and harems had lived? What would it be like, she wondered, to have all of your needs taken care of? To have your bath drawn each morning, your every need attended to? To not have to get up at dawn to go to work, to rush home and cook, to spend your weekends cleaning?

She blew a soap bubble off the tips of her fingers and laughed. This kind of a life would be fine for about a week. After that she and every other red-blooded American woman she knew would be champing at the bit. But still, for the few days that she was here, she would relax and enjoy it.

And no matter what Mike Brennan or Kumar Ben Ari said, she would go with them.

"So at last I see you again, my friend," Kumar said. "It has been too long, Brennan. I have missed you."

"And I've missed you. It's good of you to let Jenny and me stay with you, decent of you to let her stay here while I try to find her boy."

"While *we* try to find the boy, Brennan, for be assured, I am going with you. I thought you might want to rest a day or two before we leave for Al Hamaan. That is the town where the Huranis live and, undoubtedly, where they have the boy. But first, I thought that you and I might enjoy a little recreation." He winked at Brennan. "Tonight after dinner we will go into town, yes? There is a new club, La Palais Royale, where they have the most beautiful dancing girls in all of Jahan. But if the girls are not to your liking, Zahira and Maruzi will be only too glad to accommodate you. I have told them you are coming and already they are fighting over you. Perhaps we'll see them before La Palais Royale, yes?" He slapped Brennan's shoulder. "You are man enough to handle more than one woman in an evening, my brother."

"Man enough, maybe," Brennan said with a laugh, "but I'm not here for fun and games. All I want to do is concentrate on getting Jenny's son back to her."

Kumar sighed. "I see you have changed, Brennan, and I'm not sure I approve of the change. But all right, we will get the boy and *then* we will have what you call fun and games. Now you would like a drink?"

"Scotch, if you have it."

"I have it, my friend. And perhaps, since this is a special occasion, I will join you." He clapped his hands, and when a servant appeared, he ordered drinks and sweetmeats. When they were alone again, he said, "Mrs. Hurani seems to me to be a headstrong woman. That is not good, at least not here in Jahan. She'll follow orders?"

"Up to a point."

"I'll count on you to keep her in line. She must do as she is told, and she must, of course, remain behind when we go to Al Hamaan." He looked up as the servant returned with a tray, offered a glass to Mike, and took a sip of his drink before he said, "It helps that she is unattractive."

"Unattractive?"

"Well, shall we say plain? Which is good, because a man would not give her a second look."

"Oh?" Brennan smiled down at his drink.

"I thought at first, when I received your call saying you were coming to Jahan, that you had taken on this dangerous job because of the woman. I know now that cannot be true, that you are doing it only for the money."

And still Mike smiled without commenting.

"But do not worry, my friend," Kumar went on. "You will have enough feminine companionship while you are here to satisfy ten men. I will see to that."

I don't want any other women, Mike almost said. And though it was true, he wasn't sure he liked the idea of being a one-woman man. The last time he'd been here, he and Kumar had raised enough hell and partied with enough dancing girls to keep a man happy for the next thirty years. He'd always liked variety in his women. Why then did the idea of being with anyone except Jenny turn him off?

He took a long drink. The whiskey burned his throat. What the hell? he thought. Maybe he'd give the dancing girls another whirl, after all. Have a little fun with Zahira and sexy, sloe-eyed Maruzi. Sure, why not?

He sighed. He knew why not, knew that he didn't care if he never saw another dancing girl as long as he lived. The only woman he wanted was Jenny Cooper Hurani.

Once Kumar saw Jenny without the wig and glasses, he'd change his mind about her being unattractive.

And that, although he wasn't sure why, unsettled him.

Chapter 7

The two men, both of them wearing comfortable white djellabas, were half sitting, half reclining on pillowed chaises when Jenny made her appearance.

They looked like desert potentates, she thought, resisting the urge to laugh. All they needed were dancing girls with feathered fans feeding them from bunches of fat, purple grapes. It was the perfect atmosphere for Kumar Ben Ari, but for Brennan? She had the uncomfortable thought that he looked perfectly at home lolling on the pillowed silk chaise in his Arab robe, as though he had done it before, very likely with dancing girls.

They both stood when she came in. Mike smiled, but Kumar's mouth dropped open and his eyes widened with a look of utter disbelief. Instead of the dark dress and flat shoes Jenny had traveled in, she now wore the ankle-length Indian skirt she'd bought in Furnace Creek, along with the white off-the-shoulder blouse. The hated black wig was on the dresser next to the tortoiseshell glasses. Her short blond hair curled about her face. She had on eye makeup and a touch of lipstick.

"Good evening, Jenny." Mike took her hand. "Come join us. Would you care for anything to drink?"

"Yes, please." She turned to Kumar. "My rooms are lovely," she said. "Thank you."

"The—pleasure is mine." He seemed to be gasping for air.

Mike's lips twitched. "Something wrong?" he asked.

"No, I—I . . . I'm a little surprised." Kumar turned to Jenny. "The dark hair was only a wig?" he asked. "You don't need the glasses?"

She shook her head. "I know both the wig and the glasses are necessary, but I don't especially like wearing them."

"I can see why." Kumar smiled and his voice grew seductively soft. "It is a crime against nature to disguise your beauty. Your hair..." He sighed. "It is the color of wheat in the shining sun." His glance slid to her bare shoulders. "Your skin is like golden sand, your eyes the shade of the soft feathers of a dove."

He took her hand and led her to the other chaise. "Come sit down and we will have an aperitif. I have asked the cook to prepare something special for dinner this evening. I hope everything will meet with your approval."

"I'm sure it will, Mr. Ben Ari."

"Kumar," he said. "Please, you must call me Kumar." He poured champagne into a fluted crystal glass, and when he handed it to her, his fingers touched hers. "If you do not like it, if instead you would prefer something else, you need only to tell me."

She took a sip. "It's very good," she said. "Thank you."

He smiled and all but smacked his lips.

Brennan frowned. What in the hell was going on here? Kumar was one of his best friends, but by all that was holy, if he kept smiling at Jenny like a tom-cat with his eyes on a canary, Mike was going to wipe the smile right off his face.

The three of them sat down, Jenny in the middle. A robed man entered at the other end of the room, settled onto one of the oriental rugs and began to play the zither.

Kumar offered Jenny sweetmeats from the tray between them. He smiled and chatted, and all the while his dark gaze rested on her bare shoulders, her graceful neck, her lips.

Mike wanted to strangle him. But if Jenny noticed, it didn't bother her. And though he said nothing, that infuriated him all the more.

In a little while servants appeared with a variety of dishes unlike any Jenny had ever seen. There was artichoke cooked with lemon and saffron, fried eggplant with spicy Arabian sauces, honey-cooked lamb, small fish kebabs, grilled meatballs in yogurt sauce, a plate of steaming *kuskus,* zucchini stuffed with fried ground meat, spices and pine nuts. At the end of the meal, dates and nuts and a selection of eye-pleasing and mouth-watering desserts were served.

Jenny leaned back against the cushions. Because of the way she felt about Aiden, she had told herself that all Arabs were barbarians. She knew now how wrong she had been. She liked Kumar Ben Ari. It was good to know that if she and Mike ran into trouble, he might be able to help them.

He asked her about her life in California and how she had discovered Command, Inc.

"I was desperate when my ex-husband took our boy," she explained. "I had tried the police, federal agencies, anyone I could think of, but no one could help me. Then, through an article in a San Diego newspaper, I heard about Mike's group. I went to see him and he accepted my case."

"I'm not surprised that he did, but what does surprise me is that he let you come to Jahan with him."

"It's my son who is missing. Of course I would come."

"But do you realize how dangerous an undertaking it is going to be? Even though you will be sequestered here in my home while Mike and I go after your son, there is still an element of danger."

"I'm aware of the danger, Mr. Ben Ari, and please understand that I have absolutely no intention of staying behind while you and Mike go after Timmie."

"Of course you will stay behind!" He shot a look at Mike. "Tell her," he said.

"Kumar is right," he said. "You're going to stay here. Kumar and I will handle the rescue."

Anger knotted her stomach. Timmie was her son; nobody was going to keep her from going after him. She glared at both men. "I'm going," she said flatly. "That's final."

The Arabian's eyes narrowed. "If it is necessary, we will keep you here by force."

She met his gaze and narrowed her own eyes. "I'm not a Jahanian woman, Mr. Ben Ari. I will not be left behind." She stood so that she could look down at both men. "Timmie has suffered a terrible trauma by being taken away from me. Perhaps by now he's adjusted to being here with his father's family, but how do you think he'll feel if the two of you, men he's never seen before, forcefully take him away?" She shook her head. "I'm going with you," she said. "End of discussion."

"Tell her she can't," Kumar said to Mike.

Mike stood and, going to Jenny, rested his hands on her shoulders. "Do you have any idea how dangerous this is going to be?" he asked.

"I think I do."

"You're willing to risk it?"

"Of course I am." She looked into his laserlike blue eyes, then covered his hand with her own. "I have to go with you, Mike," she said in a low voice. "Please don't leave me behind."

For a moment he didn't speak, then, still looking at her, he said to Kumar, "The disguise is a good one. If she wore a robe and a veil, we could pass her off as your sister or cousin."

"That's crazy! What if we're stopped? She doesn't speak the language. She—"

"Yes, I do," Jenny said. "I was married to Aiden for six years. He insisted I speak it when his brother and father came to visit. I'm not terribly fluent, but my accent is good. I can get by."

Kumar looked past her to Brennan. "If they catch her they will kill her," he said.

"They won't catch me," Jenny said. "I'm going and that's final."

"*Zfft!*" He shouted an obscenity. "American women! You can't tell them anything!"

"You can tell us," Jenny said. "But that doesn't mean we'll listen."

"Amen to that." Brennan laughed. And it was done.

"The Huranis live in Al Hamaan," Kumar told them later, when the coffee was brought in. "It's a poor and miserable village, but the Huranis live well. They have a big house and many servants."

"How far is Al Hamaan from Zagora?" Mike asked.

"A thousand kilometers, about six-hundred miles. The trip will take two days. We'll travel by Jeep. A good bit of the trip will be through the desert." He looked at Jenny. "It will be a long, hot, uncomfortable drive. There'll be no Holiday Inns or Hilton Hotels along the road, no marble tubs or swimming pools. You won't like it."

"I don't expect to like it." Jenny met his gaze, her expression as firm and as serious as his. "I didn't come to Jahan for a vacation, Kumar, I came to get my son."

He looked at Mike and shook his head, as though to say, "What in the hell do you do with a woman like this?"

"Do you know for certain the boy is in Al Hamaan?" Mike asked.

"Yes. As soon as I had your call and knew the reason for your coming, I sent three of my men—men from my country—to Al Hamaan. They have watched the house and they report that they have seen a boy that is somewhere between four and five. We think he is Mrs. Hurani's son, but of course there is no way to be sure." He hesitated. "The boy has dark hair."

"My—my son has light hair." She touched her short curls. "Like mine," she whispered.

"That doesn't mean it isn't Timmie," Mike told her. "They've probably dyed his hair so that he wouldn't stand out among the other villagers."

"Of course," Kumar agreed. "The color of his hair is not significant. We are sure it is him."

"How can you be sure?" Jenny asked, trying to quell her rising panic and the thought that perhaps, after all, the boy wasn't Timmie.

"I have put one of my people, a woman, into the Hurani household to work as a cook. She has seen the boy and she has heard him speak a few words of English. She is sure he's an American."

Tears of relief flooded Jenny's eyes and she turned away. "I'm sorry," she whispered when she could control her voice. "It's just that there have been times when I was afraid I'd never see him again. But now I know I'll get him back." She looked appealingly at Kumar. "Is there anything else you can tell me? Is Timmie all right?"

"As far as we know, yes. I hope to receive a communication from Al Hamaan tomorrow." He took her hand and led her to the chaise. "Please be assured, *madame,* that we are doing the utmost to assure your son's safety. With the help of Allah we will restore him to you."

Once again tears rose in Jenny's eyes, her emotions were so close to the surface. "I'm so grateful to you for helping me," she said. "I don't know how I can ever thank you for what you've already done, and for what you're doing."

Kumar took her hand in his and kissed it. "I can think of many ways," he murmured.

Anger curled like a snake in Brennan's stomach. Kumar might be his best friend, but at the moment he felt an overwhelming desire to grab him by his shoulder and send him skidding over the Persian rugs. What in the hell was going on here? Jenny wasn't one of Kumar's dancing girls, she was a very special woman, a vulnerable woman. Kumar, if he knew what was good for him, had damn well better keep his hands off her. If he didn't...

His own hands clenched into fists at his sides, Mike turned to Jenny. "It's late," he snapped. "You'd better get some rest."

"Oh?" Startled by his abruptness, Jenny hesitated. Then, with a nod, she said, "Yes, I guess I should. I am a little tired."

"Then I shall send for Latife." Kumar clapped his hands, and when a manservant appeared, he said, "Tell Latife that *madame* wishes to retire."

In a moment Latife appeared, and when she did, Kumar said to Jenny, "Go along now and sleep well. If there is anything you desire you need only to ask." He looked deeply into her eyes, then took her hand and kissed it again. "Anything," he murmured.

It was all Mike could do not to go for his throat.

Jenny was puzzled. Mike had barely told her goodnight. It was obvious he was angry, but she wasn't sure why. Was he, in spite of what he'd said, upset because she had insisted in going to Al Hamaan?

Silent and thoughtful, she followed Latife through the patios and the corridors to her room. The older woman bowed Jenny inside and told her again that if she had need of anything, she had only to pick up the phone and ask.

Her bed had been turned back. A bowl of fruit had been placed on the dresser, along with an assortment of imported chocolates. Luxury, she thought. It would take some getting used to.

When she had undressed and put on her nightgown and robe, she went to stand by the open French doors that led out to the patio. The moon was full and fat and yellow. Palm fronds rustled in the slight breeze that came in off the desert, and from somewhere in the distance came the haunting cry of the muezzin calling the faithful to evening prayer.

This was a strange and foreign land, far different from what she had imagined it would be. She had come here expecting to hate all of it, yet, as she had in Death Valley, she felt a certain sense of peace. The wind off the desert was soft, the air scented with orange blossoms and jasmine.

She stepped out of her room into the night, listening to the call of the muezzin, and stood looking up at the sky.

"I thought you were tired," a voice said from the edge of darkness. And when she turned, she saw Mike standing in the shadow of the palms.

"Where—where did you come from?" she asked, startled.

"My rooms are there." He gestured off to the right. "We share the same patio."

When he stepped out of the shadows, she turned toward him, unaware that her body was clearly outlined through the sheerness of her gown. "You were angry before," she said. "Why?"

"I didn't like your flirting with Kumar."

"Flirting?" She looked at him, surprised. "I wasn't flirting."

"The hell you weren't." He started getting mad again. "Letting him kiss your hand!" He snorted. "What did you think you were doing, coming to dinner wearing that off-the-shoulder, sexy blouse?"

"It's the same blouse I wore in the desert," she said indignantly.

"That was different."

"Different? Why?" Hands on her hips, Jenny glared at him.

"Because then you were wearing it for me." He came closer. He loomed over her, tall, angry, threatening.

"Just a darn minute," Jenny said. "You can't—"

He pulled her to him. "Yes, I can," he said roughly. Then he kissed her, his mouth hard and firm against hers, stopping her protests. And when he let her go, he glared at her. "You're not in California now," he said. "You're in Arabia. The men are different here. The only women they see with naked shoulders are dancing girls or prostitutes. From now on you'll cover yourself up. Do you understand?"

Jenny pulled away from him. "I'll wear what I please," she said. "And I'll do what I please."

"The hell you will." Before she could stop him, he picked her up and carried her back into her room. And though she struggled against him, he wouldn't let her go.

"Damn you, Mike!" she cried. "Let me—"

He covered her mouth with his, stopping her words, taking her breath. His kiss was angry, defiant, possessive, because he was damned if he'd let some desert sheik, even if the sheik was the best friend he'd ever had, come on to her.

With a growl he tossed her onto the bed and came down upon her. She tried to squirm away from him, and the feel of her body through the sheerness of her gown set him on fire with an urgency unlike anything he'd ever known before.

He raised himself above her, his piercing eyes narrowed with anger and with passion. He kissed her hard, grinding his mouth against hers in a frenzy of desire. When she tried to draw away, he grasped her wrists and pinned them above her head.

"It drove me crazy," he said fiercely. "I wanted to tear him apart."

He let go of her wrists, and when he did, she saw that his fists were clenched and that his eyes burned with anger.

"Damn it," he said, "I—"

She brought her hands up to cover her face, curled herself into a ball and cried, "Don't! Don't hit me! Don't hit me!"

The color drained from his face. "Oh, my God," he whispered.

He lay beside he. She tried to shrink away from him, but he took her into his arms. Her body shook with fear; her teeth were chattering.

"Jenny," he said. "Oh, Jenny, baby." He tightened his arms around her. "Sweetheart, please don't do this. I'd never hurt you, Jenny. Don't you know that, baby?"

He kissed the eyes that were wet with tears. "I'd never lay a hand on you in anger, Jenny. I'd never hurt you."

He kissed her face, her eyes, her nose, her cheeks. And called himself every kind of a bastard because he'd frightened her. He should have known better than to have yelled at her. Her husband had beaten and abused her, and he, like some macho brute, had carried her in here and thrown her on the bed. No wonder she was frightened.

He drew her closer, continuing to murmur to her, to rain soft kisses on her face until at last she said, "I—I'm sorry, Mike. I overreacted."

"No, you didn't." He stroked her face. "I'm so sorry, Jenny. I was angry and I didn't think. But believe me, please, Jenny, believe me when I tell you that I'd never hit you in anger."

She looked at him, searching his face, her eyes so intent on his it was as though she were looking into his very soul. A sigh shivered through her; the trembling stopped. And she knew that it was true—he wasn't like Aiden. He would never hurt her.

He brushed the tousled hair back from her forehead. "I'm nuts about you," he said. "You know that, don't you?"

She smiled. "Maybe I do."

"I'd never do anything you didn't want me to do."

Something fluttered in her midsection. "What if it was something I wanted you to do?"

The breath caught in his throat. "Anything," he said. "Anything for you, Jenny."

She put her arms around his neck. "You can take my gown off now," she whispered.

He slipped it over her head, and when she lay back against the ivory satin sheet, he gazed down at her. He studied every curve and contour, her high rounded breasts, the flat stomach, the flare of hips. The legs a man could die for.

He rested a hand against her stomach. She was so soft, so fragile, so incredibly, beautifully feminine. He turned his head so that she wouldn't see the tears that stung his eyes at the thought of anyone abusing her, marring this perfect skin, wounding, causing her pain. It was more than he could bear.

He took off his robe and lay down beside her. He began to touch her with hands made gentle by all that he was feeling. He caressed her breasts, cradled her in his arms and kissed her.

"I'd never hurt you," he said against her lips.

"I know," she whispered.

"If you don't want to make love, we don't have to."

"I want to," she said.

"Ah, Jenny. My sweet Jenny."

The kiss deepened while he stroked her—her breasts, the sweet length of her body, the scented moistness between her legs. And when she said, "Please, now," he came over her and lowered himself on his arms.

"Baby," he said. "Oh, baby," and joined his body to hers.

It was a gentle coupling. He rocked her close with arms made tender by the strength of his feelings, and knew that nothing had ever been as good as the sensation of her warmth closing about him. Or of her arms holding him.

And though his body caught fire, he moved carefully, slowly against her. Only when she lifted herself to him did his movements quicken. And when they did, he took her mouth and tasted her sweetness.

She clasped his head and held him there, drinking of his mouth as he drank of hers. He was on fire with passion, but he made himself wait, wait until she said, "Mike... Oh, darling, oh, yes..."

He kissed her again, and it was as though their mouths as well as their bodies were glued together. They couldn't stop kissing, couldn't stop touching each other.

Her body moved frantically against his, and when she cried out, his voice mingled with hers and they were lost in the agonizing ecstasy of their mutual release.

In a little while he made as though to move away from her, but she wouldn't let him. They kissed and touched, and soon it began again with slow, luxurious, trancelike movements.

They whispered their pleasure into each other's mouths; they said how good this was, how perfect.

"Jen," he said against her lips. "My Jen."

As though by mutual consent, they made it last a long, long time, kissing, resting for a moment before they began to move against each other again. And when at last it was past bearing, they tightened their arms around each other and shared the quiet joy of release.

Jenny curled herself against him. She wanted to tell him how it had been for her, but she was so tired...so tired....

He kissed the top of her head and held her close. And again, as they had earlier, tears stung his eyes because she had thought he was like Aiden. And because he had begun to care for her, so much more than he ever thought he would care about anyone.

During the next two days, Kumar and Mike were gone most of the time. When Jenny did manage to see them, they had little to tell her other than that they were making arrangements for the trip to Al Hamaan.

At dinner on the third day after their arrival, Mike said, "Kumar has had word from Al Hamaan." He took her hand. "It's probably nothing to be alarmed about, Jenny, but I thought you ought to know." He looked at Kumar. "Tell her."

Kumar nodded. "The woman I have placed in the Hurani household has sent word that the boy is ill," he said.

"Ill?" Jenny stared at him. "Timmie is ill?"

"Take it easy," Mike said.

"Easy? You expect me to take it easy?" Her voice rose. "I have to go to him. He's sick. He needs me."

"Please, calm yourself," Kumar said. "He is a male child, so you can be sure he is getting the best of attention."

Frantic with concern, she turned to Mike. "I've got to get to him. I've got to get to Al Hamaan," she cried.

"The arrangements have already been made, Jenny. We leave at dawn tomorrow."

Tomorrow. Thank God. Tomorrow she would be on her way to her son.

Chapter 8

They left the city of Zagora at dawn. Jenny wore the wig, a high-necked blouse with long sleeves, a skirt that came to midcalf, black stockings and low-heeled black shoes.

The two men had been waiting for her when she walked outside to the Jeep, Mike in khaki pants and shirt, Kumar in a black djellaba. It was obvious from their expressions that they were arguing, and as she approached she heard Kumar say, "It's madness for a woman, especially an American woman, to make this trip. You should have made her stay behind."

Mike shook his head, and when he saw her, smiled and said, "I'm not sure you can make this American woman do anything she doesn't want to do, my friend."

"It will be a rough and tiring trip." Kumar sent her a ferocious frown. "The temperature will be over a hundred degrees and the Jeep is not air-conditioned. It would be better for everyone if you stayed behind."

"It wouldn't be better for me." Jenny put her small suitcase in the back of the Jeep and started to get in beside it.

"Just a minute." Mike took a holster off the front seat. "Strap this on," he said. And when she raised an eyebrow as though to ask why, he shoved a revolver into the holster and said, "We're going into danger-ous country. I want you armed."

That gave her pause. She knew there would be dan-ger once they reached Al Hamaan, but she hadn't ex-pected the trip there to be dangerous. However, she didn't question Brennan. She strapped the holster on, adjusted it around her waist and rested her hand on the hilt of the gun to get the feel of it. "Okay," she said. "I'm ready."

The first three hours on the road were a cinch. The temperature, while hot, was quite bearable, the land ruggedly beautiful. They passed villages of mud-baked houses, an occasional green oasis of sheltering palms, sedges and thorn bushes, even sections of the desert that had been transformed into fertile farmland.

"The land here is supplied with groundwater from aquifers," Kumar explained. "Though Jahan is still a poor country and primitive in many ways, it raises much of its own food and need no longer rely on other countries."

At noon, when they stopped for the lunch they had brought with them, Jenny asked where they would spend the night. "Is there a town between here and Al Hamaan?" she said.

"There's a village," Kumar said. "And an inn of sorts. But it isn't a place you would wish to stay." He bit into a date. "We'll camp on the desert. It will be cleaner and far less dangerous."

Jenny looked at him inquiringly, then at Brennan. So there really was a reason why she had to wear the gun. This wasn't cops-and-robbers pretend. Both men were deadly serious.

"Not many foreigners come to Jahan," Mike said. "Those who do are usually connected with the oil companies. When I was here before it was as Kumar's guest. It's different in a city like Zagora, but even there you see very few foreign men, and almost no Western women. Those who are there are traveling with their husbands."

"In the smaller villages it is *haram*, forbidden, for a woman, especially one who is not robed or veiled, to travel alone," Kumar said. "Here in Jahan, as well as in a few other Middle Eastern countries, a woman cannot board a plane without written permission from a male relative. Her modesty is always zealously guarded. It's never wise for any woman, especially a foreigner, to assume she can do as she pleases in a country like this."

He hesitated, as though debating what he thought he should tell her, then said, "Last year a French woman came to Jahan to take photographs for the magazine she worked for. In spite of repeated warnings, she insisted on traveling to remote villages with only her driver. She wore trousers, which is considered *haram*, and makeup, also *haram*."

He looked at Mike and raised a questioning eyebrow.

"Go ahead," Mike said. "Tell her."

"She stayed overnight in one of the villages we passed this morning. The next morning her driver found her savagely beaten. Her clothes had been ripped off and she had been raped repeatedly. Her camera and film had been destroyed.''

"Was she—" Jenny wet her lips "—was she alive?"

"Barely. The driver managed to get her to a hospital in Zagora. An official from the magazine she worked for flew in, and as soon as she was able to travel, he took her back with him.'' Kumar reached for an orange and began to peel it. "So yes, Jenny, there is danger.''

"That's why as soon as we reach Al Hamaan, you're going to be robed and veiled,'' Mike said. "You'll be a Jahanian woman, a relative of Kumar's. You'll walk five paces behind us and you will not lift your head unless you're spoken to.''

"Oh, come *on!*" Jenny started to laugh, but the laughter died in her throat when she saw the expression on Mike's face. "You're really serious,'' she said.

He nodded. "I told you when we left California that you could come with me only if you followed orders, Jenny. And that's what you're going to do. If you think Kumar made up the story about the French woman to scare you, you're mistaken. It happened. Jahan has its own customs, its own laws.''

"As well as desert bandits,'' Kumar said. "Which is why as soon as we reach the more remote sections of the country, we must keep a careful lookout.''

"Bandits?'' She looked at him unbelievingly.

"Bandits who could live for a year on what they would get for selling the Jeep and the things we carry,'' Mike said. "Tonight when we camp, Kumar and I will take turns standing guard.''

They left the place where they had stopped for lunch. The temperature climbed, the fertile farmland disappeared and the pavement gave way to a dirt road. The dust and heat were suffocating; the landscape became scorched and hostile. There was only sand for as far as they could see, a chain of great dunes that stretched unbroken into the vast wilderness. By three that afternoon the temperature had risen to over a hundred and ten degrees.

Mike and Kumar took turns driving. Every once in a while Mike turned around to ask, "Are you all right?"

"Fine," Jenny said each time he asked. "Fine."

Death Valley had been bad, but this was worse. She was uncomfortable, miserable and dirty. Her head was burning under the wig, sweat dripped down between her breasts, and though she took frequent sips of water, her throat was parched, her lips already cracked.

She kept telling herself that every mile brought her closer to Timmie. He had crossed this same desert, suffered this same heat. The thought of that—of how frightened he must have been, how bewildered by what was happening—made her more determined than ever to take him away from Aiden.

She gazed out at the terrible desolation. Waves of heat shimmered from the desert floor. There weren't even any desert animals or birds. Why had Aiden, who'd held a good job in San Diego, wanted to return to this godforsaken country? Had he hated her so much that he was willing to risk their son's life by bringing him here?

When had it started? she wondered as she gazed out at the barren landscape. What had changed Aiden from the young man she had known at college to the cold and abusive man he had become? Had he always been like that or had the arrival of his father and brother from Jahan made him so different?

She had been pleased when he'd told her they were coming for a visit. She'd cleaned the house from top to bottom, and that first evening had cooked a special dish she'd found in a Middle Eastern cookbook at the library.

Nothing had pleased them. After she had served and started to sit down at the table, his father, a large man with heavy features, a mustache and a short-trimmed chin beard, had raised his thick eyebrows and in a disapproving voice said, "You allow your woman to eat with you?"

"It is the custom in the United States for a wife to sit at the table with her husband," Aiden had answered.

"You may be in the United States, but you are Jahanian." Tamar Ben Hurani had shaken his head. "You forget our ways, my son. That saddens me. I can see that we must talk."

She had looked uncertainly from Aiden to his father. Then Aiden had said, "You will eat after we have finished, Jenny."

The whole time that his father and brother were there, she had been treated like a servant. She had disliked Aiden's father and she had feared his brother.

A few years older than Aiden, Mustafa stood a head taller. He was handsome in a blunt and brutish way. His hands were large, the backs of them covered with a thick mat of black hair.

He watched her all the time, and each night when Aiden returned home from work, Mustafa would take him aside and with glances her way speak in Jahanian, too fast for her to understand. Later, when they were alone in their room, Aiden would say, "You went next door to Mrs. Miller's today. You were gone for forty-five minutes. What did you do there?"

The first time it had happened, Jenny had stared at him, unable to believe that he was serious. And when she had realized he *was* serious, she'd told him he was acting like a suspicious fool. That was the first time he had hit her.

Two days later she had gone to lunch with Josie McCall. Josie had moved to Washington, D.C., right after graduation to work for the International Health Organization. She'd come to San Diego on business and Jenny had been delighted to see her again. They'd had a three-hour lunch and talked, as best friends do, of old times and of what was happening in their lives. Jenny thought later that Josie had detected her unhappiness, but all that she'd said before they parted was, "If you ever need to talk, you know that I'm here for you."

When Jenny returned home, Mustafa had been waiting for her.

"Go to your room at once," he'd shouted.

Timmie had looked from his uncle to Jenny. He'd clutched Jerry Giraffe around its long neck and, starting to cry, he'd run toward Jenny.

Mustafa had stopped him. He'd pulled the toy out of Timmie's arms. "Stop acting like a baby," he'd said, and thrown the toy animal across the room. Before Jenny could go to her son, he'd grabbed her, opened her bedroom door, shoved her inside and locked the door behind her.

She could hear Timmie crying. That was worse than the humiliation and the rage of being treated like a prisoner in her own home—to know that her son needed her and that she couldn't go to him.

That night when Aiden returned she told him what had happened. Instead of giving her the support she expected, he had berated her. And told her she was never again to go out without his permission.

She had thought that it would be better after Mustafa and Aiden's father left, but it hadn't been. Everything she did displeased Aiden. He had beaten and abused her, and finally she had left him. And because he could no longer control her, he had kidnapped their child and taken him out of the country.

The heat and the dust didn't matter. She was here now and she would do whatever she had to do to get Timmie back, because he was her child and she loved him with all her heart.

And because the thought of his being raised the way Aiden and Mustafa had been, believing that women were merely servants to men, filled her with a rage unlike anything she had ever known. He was *her* little boy. She was damned if he was going to grow up in the image of his father.

They camped that night in the lee of a sand dune. Since lunch they had passed no other vehicle. Once in the distance they'd seen a small caravan of camels, but for the last few hours there had been no one.

Mike built a fire and they prepared a simple meal of *kuskus* and flat bread. Over coffee, he said, "I'll take the first watch, Kumar. You get some sleep."

"I'm not tired yet, my friend. I'll sit with you awhile." He looked over at Jenny, who could barely keep her eyes open. "It's better that you rest," he said.

"It will be even hotter tomorrow than it has been to-day."

"How long will it take us to get to Al Hamaan from here?" she asked.

"Nine or ten hours. If we leave at dawn we should arrive in the early afternoon. It would be best if to-morrow you wore the robe."

"But I thought I wouldn't have to do that until we got to Al Hamaan," she protested. "It's bad enough wearing a dress, but I'll swelter in a robe."

"Actually, it will be cooler than what you wore to-day. You won't have to put the veil on until we near Al Hamaan."

She turned to Mike for support, but he only nod-ded and said, "Kumar's right. Tomorrow you wear the robe."

She bit back a retort, said a brief good-night and went to the small, one-man tent they had set up for her. Every bone in her body ached from the hours she'd spent bouncing around in the back seat of the Jeep. She was hot and dusty, but she knew better than to ask for water to bathe. She took off the skirt and blouse and put on her nightgown.

As tired as she was, she couldn't find a comfort-able position. From outside the tent came the low voices of the two men. She closed her eyes and was just rounding the corner of sleep when she heard Kumar say, "So, my friend, tell me. Is there something seri-ous going on between you and the woman?"

"I'm not sure I know what you mean," Mike said.

"Oh, come now. She's very beautiful, yes? Stub-born and determined to have her own way, but still a woman to turn any man's head. The two of you have been traveling together. You're very protective of her. I thought perhaps..." Kumar chuckled. "You know."

"No, I don't know. Jenny's a client. She hired me to get her son back and that's what I'm going to do."

"Then you are not emotionally involved?"

There was a moment of silence, then Mike said, "No, of course not. It's all strictly business between Jenny and me."

Jenny swallowed hard and fought to hold back the tears. He sounded so cold, so matter-of-fact. Hadn't the special moments they had shared meant anything to him? Was it, after all, strictly business, with a little lovemaking on the side to ease the stress?

She punched her pillow, then buried her face in it so they wouldn't hear her crying.

She awoke to the sound of gunfire. Before she came fully awake, Mike had thrown open the tent flap. "Bandits!" he cried. "Stay where you are."

She rolled to a sitting position and reached for the gun she had taken off before she'd lain down last night. On her hands and knees, clutching the holster and bullets, she crawled out of the tent, and almost screamed in terror.

In the light of early dawn she saw men on horseback riding full speed at them, firing as they came. Mike and Kumar were behind the Jeep, rifles ready, taking aim. Jenny ran toward the vehicle and fell to her knees behind a wheel.

"Stay down!" Mike yelled at her.

She raised her gun and fired at the horseman nearest to her. He clutched his chest and fell. She fought the momentary weakness in her stomach, a stab of horror and revulsion, and kept firing.

"Bravo!" Kumar cried. Then he, too, brought a man down.

But still they came, crying their savage cries, plunging forward on their horses, faces half-covered by the hooded burnooses they wore. It was like a scene out of hell—the terrible, shrieking cries of the bandits, the sounds of gunfire, the whine of bullets. No time to think only to fire and reload, fire and reload.

One of them leapt over the Jeep. Jenny whirled, smelling the horse and human sweat, and saw the bandit level his rifle at Mike. Before she could cry out, Kumar fired and the man, his eyes wide and blank, fell without a sound.

Bullets spit sand close to where Jenny crouched, but she kept firing. She didn't know how long it went on before a cry went up and the remaining bandits turned their horses and headed away from the camp, out toward the desert.

"They're going. Praise Allah." Kumar looked at Brennan. "You're all right?"

"Yeah, thanks to you." Mike wiped the dirt and sweat off his face before he glowered down at Jenny and said, "Dammit, woman, I told you to stay where you were."

"Thank Allah that she did not." Kumar went to her and took her hands. "You were wonderful, Jenny. We needed that extra gun and you're a remarkable shot. If all American women are like you, then I, Kumar Ben Ari, praise Allah for them."

She smiled her thanks before she looked over his shoulder at Mike. His jaw was clenched, his eyes hot with anger before he turned away and started rolling up his and Kumar's bedrolls. "Come on!" he said. "We've got to get out of here before they come back."

He swung back to Jenny, glowering. "Cover yourself," he snapped.

She realized then that she was still in her nightgown and that very likely her body was pretty clearly outlined. She blushed, and when she did, Kumar took her hand and said, "I would not like to be awakened by bandits every morning, but I think this morning it was worth it." He kissed her hand. "You are a remarkable woman, Miss Jenny. As brave as you are beautiful."

"Get dressed!" Mike roared. "What in the hell do the two of you think this is, a picnic? Maybe the men who attacked us are part of a bigger group. Maybe they've just ridden off for reinforcements. We've got to get the hell out of here."

"You're right, my friend." Kumar smiled at Jenny, kissed her hand again and let her go.

She smiled back, and pretended that she did not hear Mike swearing under his breath.

The robe covered her from neck to ankle, but it was loose, and cooler than she would have thought.

She'd had little to say to Brennan, or he to her since they had left camp. Now and then he turned to look at her, and each time he did she looked away.

They stopped again at noon to fill the gas tank from one of the tins they had brought with them, and prepared a simple meal in the shade of an outcrop of rocks. The temperature was well over a hundred and twenty. The air was still, the sky the bluest blue Jenny had ever seen.

"I'm going to climb the dune and have a look around," Kumar said when they finished eating. "I won't be long."

They watched him scramble up the sloping sand, a dark figure in his black djellaba, and when he was out of earshot, Mike said, "Okay, what in the hell's going on?"

"I don't know what you mean." Jenny turned away from him and started clearing up the remains of their lunch.

"Don't give me that, Jen." He took her arm and brought her around to face him. "Are you upset because I yelled at you this morning? Is that it? If it is, you must know I did it because I was afraid for you, because I didn't want anything to happen to you."

"Afraid you might lose your client, Brennan?"

He stared down at her, surprised. "What are you talking about? I don't..." He stopped, muttered an oath, then said. "You heard what I said to Kumar last night, about your just being a client, didn't you?"

"Yes, I heard. And it's okay, Brennan, I understand." Her voice was cold as ice. "Give the little lady a romp in the sack. Kinda eases the tension when things get rough, doesn't it? And if she's not too bad, it's a little bonus for you. Right?"

His face went red, then white, and his blue eyes glittered with anger. He took a step toward her, and before she could move, he pulled her closer. "Wrong," he said. "Dead wrong. I said what I did last night because I didn't think you'd want Kumar to know what had been going on between us. Because I thought that what we shared was too good to talk about. If you can't understand that, I sure as hell am not going to take the time to explain it to you."

"Let me go!"

He pulled her closer. "I've told you before, I don't like you flirting with Kumar. So stop it or—"

"Or what?" she challenged.

She was so close he could feel the outline of her body against his. He saw the thin film of sweat on her forehead and smelled the desert heat on her skin. She didn't flinch or try to move away; she only stood there, her chin thrust out, gray eyes blazing into his, challenging him as he challenged her.

He gripped her shoulders. "Or I'll kiss you until your eyes bulge and your nose bleeds," he sputtered. "I'll take you behind the nearest sand dune and love the ever-lovin' stuffing out of you. I'll—"

Her body softened under his hands. "Promises, promises," she said.

"Dammit, Jenny—"

She stood on her tiptoes and brushed a quick kiss across his mouth before she stepped away from him. "I get the message," she said. "But you're right, about me being your client, I mean. I honestly think it would be better, at least for now, if we kept this a strictly professional relationship."

His expression looked almost as ferocious as it had a few moments ago, but she went on before he could stop her.

"The important thing now, the reason we're here, is to get Timmie back. I only want to think about him. He's the one you should be thinking about, too."

"If that's the way you want it."

"For now," Jenny said.

He stepped away from her. "Okay, Jen. But when this is over..." He let the words hang.

"We'll see," she said. "We'll see."

Chapter 9

They stopped on the outskirts of Al Hamaan so that Jenny could put her veil on. The material, of a heavy black gauze, was held by an inch-wide band low over her forehead. It fell, with a slit barely wide enough for her to see through, to just below her throat.

It was hard to believe that there were women in a great part of the world who, except in the presence of their immediate families, had worn a veil for most of their lives. Men here made the laws and women had no choice but to obey. And though this was a charade she had to play only for this particular period of time, it rankled.

Kumar looked her over carefully. "Yes," he said at last, "it will do. It would be impossible to tell you from an Arabian woman, even with your gray eyes." He hesitated and with a frown added, "However, even veiled and robed it is possible to tell you are beautiful, and that worries me. There is a saying from the

Koran that reads, 'Say to the believing women that they cast down their eyes.' Now I believe it should read, 'Say to the *beautiful* women.'" A smile quirked the corners of his mouth. "Mike and I must be careful of you, Jenny, for if we are not, I fear a man with the hot blood of the desert Bedouins will steal you away from us."

"Over my dead body," Mike said, so emphatically they both stared at him, startled.

"Do not look so ferocious, my friend," Kumar said with a laugh. "I was only joking."

But was it a joke? Jenny wondered. The three of them were walking into a dangerous, life-threatening situation. They had to be careful, she especially, because if she gave herself away, if she uttered one word of English, it could be fatal, not only for her, but for Mike and Kumar as well. Mike had said earlier that it would mean prison for himself and Kumar, but now she knew that they, as well as she, would face death if they were caught.

Still, it was incomprehensible to her that Aiden, if he discovered that she was here in Al Hamaan, would stand by and see her killed. They had been married for six years, and in the beginning she had thought that he loved her. She did not know what had changed that love. Perhaps it had been the coming of his father and Mustafa, their insistence of the old ways of his country. But she could not believe that even after all that had passed, there was not something, some memory of the earlier days when they had been happy left between them. She was the mother of his child—surely he still felt some sense of honor, some remnant of feeling because together they had created their son.

But Mustafa? A chill of foreboding ran through her. Mustafa was dangerous, deadly. So deadly that if he discovered her identity, nothing could protect her.

He had told her once when they were alone that Aiden was too easy on her. "If you were my woman," he had said, "you would do exactly as I say or suffer the consequences." He had lowered his head so that his face was only inches from hers. His lips were wet and moist, his eyes filled with a heated lust that frightened her so much she could barely breathe. "If it were not for Aiden, I would make you my wife," he'd said. "Believe me that within a month, if I told you to crawl to me on your hands and knees, you would crawl."

"Let me go!" she had cried. "I'll tell Aiden—"

His laugh had cut off her words. "Aiden acts like a weak puppy where you're concerned, but he will learn, because I will teach him, that he is the master of his household and that your only purpose is to do his bidding. He is a Jahanian man. It is time he acted like one."

A Jahanian man. She had never forgotten his words, or that on that day she had resolved that her son would not grow up like his father or Mustafa. She would do whatever she had to to prevent that. That's why she was here; she would get her son back or she would die trying.

The town of Al Hamaan lay on the crest of a hill, a cluster of dun-colored buildings among some scattered palms and oil rigs.

As they came closer, the road became clogged with camels. The riders looked at them and the Jeep with curiosity. It was obvious that very few strangers ever came to Al Hamaan.

"Keep your eyes lowered," Mike said under his breath. "Don't appear curious."

Jenny was curious, and so anxious to arrive she could barely control herself. But she did as she was told, casting only surreptitious glances at the high stone walls that surrounded the town and the turreted tower that Kumar said had been used in the olden days to warn the people of Al Hamaan of invaders.

They passed through the Moorish arches into the noisy, bustling section where camels, donkeys and bicycles crowded the dusty streets. Black-clad and veiled women, like a flock of silent crows, moved among the market stalls. Men in striped djellabas, white robes, black robes, with *howlis* or fezzes covering their heads, hurried through the street.

There were children, too—little boys who scampered amid the market stalls, crying out to one another, tossing a ball or an orange back and forth or playing tag. Was there one among them with lighter skin and hair as blond as hers? Did her child ever play here? Did any of the boys know him?

She wanted to get out of the Jeep, to stop them and ask, "Do you know my son? Tamar Hurani? Do you know him?"

It was agony to be here in the town where he was, agony to wait when her heart cried out to him, "Timmie...Timmie."

A line of camels passed in front of them, saddles festooned with bright tassels. Their riders, robed men with head coverings, swayed with the movement of the beasts.

Above the hubbub of the throng came the tinny sound of music, of drums and pipes and ancient strings. Mingled with it came the notes of a flutelike instrument, and when Jenny looked, she saw a snake charmer no more than five feet from the Jeep, the thick cobra body with its flat head swaying to the eerie music the man played.

They drove slowly, past open stalls that displayed all manner of tin work: lanterns, pots and plates, pitchers and cone-shaped incense burners. And other stalls with wallets and belts, slippers and sandals, silver necklaces, caftans and robes, rugs and tapestries. Fruit stands, colorful with pomegranates, oranges and lemons and tangerines, purple grapes, green grapes, melons, bananas and mangoes, lined the road.

Carcasses of skinned and bloody cows hung from meat hooks in front of an open-stall butcher shop. A squealing pig was tied to a post nearby.

The air was permeated with the smell of grilled chicken, frying sausage, mutton, camel dung, rose water and incense, cinnamon and mint, oregano and basil, cloves, chili, garlic and ginger.

A man draped with bright red cloth festooned with gold cups, and bells strung around his neck, moved among the throng ringing a bell and crying, "*L'ma, l'ma,* water, water."

It was a strange and foreign land, filled with exotic sights and sounds and smells. But it was a dangerous land. There was no embassy here, no refuge.

When they stopped to let a string of donkeys pass in front of them, a dark-robed man looked at them with obvious suspicion.

"We are looking for the house of Youssef Madih," Kumar said. "Can you direct us?"

The man rubbed a grizzled chin. "Madih the dye-maker?"

Kumar nodded. "He is my cousin. I have come for a visit."

The look of suspicion faded. "Go to the end of the street, past the mosque. Then you must follow to your left until you reach the edge of town. There you will find the house of Madih." He looked curiously at Brennan, but didn't even glance in Jenny's direction.

"Shukran," Kumar said. *"Salâm alêkom,* peace be upon you, friend."

"Alêkom-os-salâm, and upon you peace," came the answer.

The donkey passed and they moved on.

"Is that where we'll stay?" Mike asked. "With this fellow Madih?"

Kumar nodded. "He and I have had other dealings. He has the right connections and he will help us, as long as the price is right. My men are with him and the three of us will stay at his home until we have the boy. Madih is skilled in the art of forgery and will make the exit papers for Jenny's son."

They made their way slowly down the crowded thoroughfare, then turned onto a cobblestone street. At the end of it, almost at the edge of town, they reached a dun-colored wall. In the middle was an arched entryway.

"This must be it." Kumar parked the Jeep. "Wait here," he said, and went to knock on the blue door.

A bell jingled from somewhere inside and in a moment or two an elderly woman opened the door.

"Mesa al khair," Kumar said. "Good evening. Is this the house of Youssef Madih?"

She looked at him, then past him toward the Jeep. "There is an entrance farther down. I will have the gate opened. It is best you enter there."

"*Shukran*," Kumar said with a nod. He drove to where the woman had indicated, and when the portal swung back, he nosed the Jeep inside.

"Prince Kumar!" the man who had opened the portal called out. "*Labas?* How are you? We have been expecting you."

"Greetings, Yassir. All goes well?"

"Well enough." The man was in his early twenties. He had thick black eyebrows, eyes so dark they were almost black, and instead of a djellaba, he wore dark pants and a sweatshirt. He glanced toward Brennan and Jenny.

"My friends," Kumar said. "Mr. Mike Brennan from the United States, and the woman I told you about."

"Mrs. Hurani. Yes." Yassir touched his fingertips to his forehead and bowed. "We have been awaiting your arrival, *sidi, madame*. If you will come this way please."

They entered the courtyard of what looked like a middle-class house. There was a smaller center fountain with a few scraggly plants and shrubs, date palms and a wealth of decorative tilework. Yassir motioned them through another arched entryway. Here there was a larger patio, with blue doors opening off it.

"I will have a servant show *madame* to her room," Yassir said. "Then we will talk."

"I prefer to be in on any discussion you might have," Jenny said.

The thick dark eyebrows rose. The young man looked at Kumar in surprise.

"Mrs. Hurani is an American," Kumar said, as though that explained everything. "She's very anxious to learn about her son, so perhaps it would be best if she joined us."

"As you wish, *sidi*." Young Yassir looked at Jenny, and with a shake of his head motioned for the three of them to follow him.

They went into a small room. Three men sat on the floor around a low table, but when they saw Kumar, they stood and, touching their fingers to their foreheads, bowed. One of them said, "Prince Ben Ari. Praise Allah that you have arrived safely."

"*Shukran,* Omar."

"You had no trouble?"

"A few bandits. Nothing more."

"Allah is good."

"These are my friends," Kumar said. "Mr. Mike Brennan and the woman who was the wife of Aiden Hurani. Mike, Jenny, this is my right-hand man, Omar Ben Ismail. The short, fat fellow who needs a shave is Abdur. The gentleman in the white robe is our host, Youssef Madih."

"Gentlemen," Mike said, and offered his hand.

"My house is your house, Mr. Brennan." A man of middle age, his eyes hidden behind dark glasses, acknowledged Mike before he turned to Jenny and said, "One of my wives will show you to your room, *madame*."

"Mrs. Hurani is anxious to learn about her son, Mr. Madih," Mike explained. "She would like to be a part of the discussion before she retires."

Madih's frown was so ferocious his wide mustache trembled. "It is for the men to discuss," he said.

Jenny's chin firmed. In the careful Jahanian she had learned from Aiden, she said, "I appreciate your hospitality, Mr. Madih. It is most kind of you to allow us into your home, but I really must insist that I know everything that's going on."

Ignoring her, he said to Kumar, "She is your woman?"

Kumar shook his head. "No, Madih, she is not my woman. However, Mr. Brennan is a friend of mine. Because of our friendship I have offered to help Mrs. Hurani find her son." He smiled. "She is a most determined woman. It would be best to let her know what is going on."

Madih grunted. "Most unusual," he muttered. "Most unusual."

The seven of them sat around the low table. Madih clapped his hands and a woman, swathed in a black robe, a veil and a head covering, entered. "We will have tea, Fatima," he said. "And something to eat. Our guests have traveled far today and have need of refreshment."

The woman bowed. In a voice barely above a whisper she murmured, "Yes, *sidi.*"

Three of the men lit cigarettes. It was warm in the room, and close. Jenny took off the scarf that covered the wig, and after a moment's hesitation took the wig off and ran her fingers through her short blond hair. There came a murmuring of surprise from the men gathered around the table. She started to remove her veil, but before she could, Kumar put a cautioning hand on her arm.

"No," he said in English. "That would not be acceptable."

She hesitated, torn between saying, "What nonsense," and the knowledge that as long as she was a guest here, she would have to abide by the rules. She would do anything she had to do, humble herself in any way, if only these men would help get her son back.

Speaking slowly in Jahanian, in a low and courteous voice, she said, "I am most anxious to learn the whereabouts of my son."

"He is not too far from here," Omar Ben Ismail said before turning to Kumar. "The Hurani house is three kilometers out of town on the road leading to Quasam. The house is large and well guarded. It will be difficult to get into, but not impossible. We have placed a man inside the grounds as a gardener, and Seferina, who has worked with us before, is in the kitchen."

"What news of my son? He has been ill. I want to know how he is."

"The boy has recovered from his illness," Yassir said. "He is well again. You must rest your mind on this, *madame.*"

"Thank you, Yassir," Jenny said gratefully.

"Our man saw him only yesterday," Abdur said. "He was in the garden with one of the guards."

"The boy is guarded?" Mike asked.

Omar nodded. "Most of the time. It will not be easy to get to him. Or to get out of the house once we have him."

"When can we do it?" Jenny asked.

"We?" Madih shook his head. "The men will decide when and how it is to be done."

"But he's my son," Jenny protested. "I have to—"

"When we have decided how this is to be handled, we'll tell you," Mike said in English.

She glared at him and, caution forgotten, sputtered, "I insist on knowing what's going on."

"You'll know when you need to. Remember where we are and who we're with. Now be quiet and let the men do the talking."

She was so mad she wanted to yank off the veil, stamp her foot and declare that she was an American woman and that she would not, by God, be told to sit quietly by while men did the talking and planning. She actually had her hand on the veil when she caught Mike's warning look. His eyes were serious. He was trying to tell her that if she wanted the cooperation of these Jahanian men, she had better mind her manners. And though it cost her, she lowered her eyes and said, in her slow Jahanian, "Please forgive my being so impetuous, gentlemen. It is my worry over my son that has made me behave so badly."

"Of course, *madame*," Yassir said. "We understand. Believe me, we are here to help and to protect you. We will do whatever is necessary, risk whatever must be risked, to get your son safely back to you."

"*Shukran*, Yassir. I know I can count on you."

He swallowed and hot color rose in his face. "Indeed you can," he murmured. "I am here to serve you."

The woman returned. She placed a pot of hot mint tea on the table, along with flat bread, grilled lamb kebabs, a bowl of fruit and dates.

The men began to talk, most of the time in Jahanian too swift for Jenny to understand. She sipped her tea and remained silent. When the meal was finished, Kumar said, slowly enough so that she could understand, "Tonight we will speak to the man and the woman we have placed inside the Hurani household. Then we will decide when to go in."

She clenched her hands together under the table. "Will I be able to speak to them?" Her voice grew husky, her emotions close to the surface. "Please, Kumar, speak to Mr. Madih for me. Explain how worried I am. How desperately I want to know everything I can about Timmie."

"I understand, Jenny, and I will arrange it. Now it is best that you go to your room. Someone will come for you when it is time."

He said something to Youssef Madih. The other man nodded, then clapped his hands, and in a few moments the same woman who had brought the dinner entered.

"Take the lady to her room," he ordered. "She is not to leave until she is sent for."

And though Jenny had to bite her tongue, she managed to nod her head and as humbly as she could murmur, "*Shukran,* Youssef Madih. I'm grateful for your kindness."

Mike rose with her, and when they had moved a little away from the others, he said in a voice low enough so no one could hear, "I know this is hard on you, Jenny, but you have to understand that we're in a different world here. Madih is taking a great risk by having us in his home, and Kumar is putting his and his men's lives on the line by helping us. We're all of us going to do everything we can to get your boy away from the Huranis, but you have to be patient and let us work this out."

She took a deep breath. "I know, Mike, and I'm sorry. It's just that now we're here, so close to Timmie . . .'' Tears filled her eyes and for a moment she couldn't speak. When she did, she said, ''It's hard to wait. I want to go storming into the Hurani house and grab him up in my arms and take him as far away from here as I can get.''

''I know.'' He rested a hand on her shoulder. More than anything in the world right now he wanted to take her in his arms, to comfort and hold her and promise her that everything was going to be all right and that soon she would have her son back with her.

The other men were watching them. ''Until later then,'' he said. ''Go now.'' And she turned to follow the woman out the door.

Once she had closed the door, the woman pointed to herself and said, ''Fatima. Wife of Madih.''

''I am Geneva.''

''Wife of Aiden Hurani.''

Jenny shook her head. ''No longer. We are divorced.''

''Ahh. And he has taken his son.''

''Our son. My son.''

''But he is the father. It is his right.''

''I have my rights, too.''

Fatima shook her head. ''Our husbands are our lords, *madame*. We have only to please and to obey.''

''But I'm not Jahanian, Fatima.''

They moved farther down the corridor. ''What is it like to be an American woman?'' Fatima asked. ''If you do not have a husband to protect you, what do you do?''

''I have a job,'' Jenny said. ''I drive myself to work every morning and I—''

''You are allowed to drive a car?''

"Of course." Jenny looked at her more closely. "Can't Jahanian women drive?"

"Why would we want to when we can have a man drive us?" Fatima shook her head. "Besides, *madame,* it is *haram* for a woman to drive."

"I see. But it's different in America, Fatima. In America a woman can do a lot of things. She can work in any job she's qualified for and support herself so that she doesn't have to depend on a man to take care of her. She can run for political office and have a say in how things are run."

"Politics? A say in things? But why would she want to when it is easier to let a man take charge?" Fatima shook her head in amazement. "And you may dress as you choose? There is no such a thing as a veil?"

"No such thing," Jenny said, and smiled because the idea of telling an American woman she had to wear a veil boggled the mind. She looked at the other woman curiously. "Do you wear your veil even when you're at home?"

"Not if I am with only the family. But if there are other men here, as there are now, then I, as well as the other women in the household, must be veiled."

"That doesn't bother you?"

Fatima shook her head. "I have worn the veil since I was ten, *madame.* It is a part of my wardrobe, a part of who I am." She opened a door and stepped back to let Jenny enter. "We are very different," she said.

"In some ways, perhaps. But we are both women, Fatima. Yes?"

The eyes behind the veil softened. "Yes, *madame.* I, too, have children, and I am sorry about your son. I pray to Allah he will be returned to you."

"*Shukran,* Fatima."

The other woman nodded, then, as silently as a black shadow, turned and went back down the dimly lighted corridor. And Jenny went inside the room.

It was far different than her suite of rooms at Kumar's. It was small. The window that looked out onto a dusty patio was the size of a shoe box. There was room enough for a small bed, a straight-backed chair and a dresser. A single light bulb hung from the ceiling. The bathroom, barely large enough to squeeze into, held a toilet and a sink. There was no mirror above the sink.

Jenny took off the veil and sat down on the bed. It was hard; the bed springs squeaked. It didn't matter. Nothing mattered, because she was here in Al Hamaan and tomorrow or the next day or the day after that she would be with Timmie.

She got up and went to the travel bag she had put on the chair when she entered. She took the orange giraffe out of the bag and, clutching it to her, went back to the bed and lay down and pressed the ragged animal to her breast. "Timmie," she whispered, comforted by the sound of his name in the quiet of the room.

"I want to talk to you," Kumar said once he and Mike were alone. "About Jenny."

Mike nodded. "Sure. Go ahead."

"I asked you on the trip here if there was something going on between the two of you. You told me it was strictly business. Now I am wondering if you were speaking the truth."

Mike frowned. "Why?"

"I find her attractive. She is a woman of spirit and of great courage. She is also beautiful—too independent, of course, but that could be controlled. If, as you say, there is nothing of a personal nature between the two of you, then perhaps I have a chance with her. If you have no interest, I intend to do everything I can to win her."

Mike shook his head. "Forget it!" he said. "Just forget it."

"But you said she was merely a client. Why should you care whether or not I make my move?"

Mike took a deep breath. "Because I lied," he said. "Because I'm crazy about her." He looked at his friend. "But it scares the hell out of me, Kumar, because I'm not sure I'm ready for a commitment. I know I'm not ready for fatherhood."

"A woman like Jenny comes along once in a lifetime. If you let her go..." Kumar shrugged. "If you let her go, my friend, and you lose her, then you have no one to blame but yourself." He turned away, but at the door he stopped and looked back at Mike. "Think about it," he said. "Because if you do not want her, I do."

Chapter 10

It was after nine when Fatima came to summon her. Jenny had slept for a little while, then bathed and washed her hair as best she could in the tiny bathroom before she changed into a clean white robe. She put the black veil on, but did not cover her hair.

The men were in a different room tonight. Only Mike, Yassir and Kumar stood when she entered. The others merely looked up at her, their expressions curious, hostile. She was an outsider, an infidel who spoke up to give opinions that weren't asked for. They had a job to do and they would do it, but they didn't like the idea that a woman had tried to tell them what to do.

"This is Bouchaib." Kumar indicated one of the men sitting on the floor. "He works as a gardener in the Hurani household and he is one of us."

Jenny nodded. *"Mesa al khair,"* she said by way of a greeting.

"Mesa annour," Bouchaib answered.

"And this is Seferina, the woman we have placed in the Hurani kitchen."

Middle-aged and heavy, the woman wore a dark robe, a head covering and a veil.

Jenny held out her hand. "What can you tell me of my son?" she asked.

"He is a good boy," Seferina said. "But quiet. And sad, I think."

Little boy lost, little boy sad. She fought for control. "I heard that he had been ill. Is he better now?"

"Yes, *madame.*"

"What was wrong with him?"

"An infection of the stomach. He could keep nothing down. I heard from one of the servants that when the boy was ill and his father wanted to send for the doctor, the older brother, Mustafa, said he should not coddle the boy. Finally a doctor was called, but by then the child was very weak. It has taken him a long time to recover."

Jenny clasped her hands together to keep them from trembling. The news that her child had been ill, that he might have died had a doctor not been sent for, devastated her. She ached to see him, to hold him in her arms and know for herself that he was all right. If only there was a way she could get into the house. If only... She hesitated, then said to Seferina, "Are there others besides you who work in the kitchen?"

"No, *madame,* there is only myself. A manservant serves the table. There has been talk of getting another woman to help me in the kitchen, but nothing has been done."

"What if—" Jenny took a deep breath "—what if a relative of yours, a sister or a cousin, were to come from a neighboring village to help you?"

Seferina shook her head. "I have no sister. Yassir is my only cousin."

"But what if—"

"Forget it!" Mike said in English.

"It would work," Jenny said. "I know it would."

"Listen!" He felt himself getting angry, tried to hold it back and couldn't. "I've let you come this far against my better judgment," he snapped, "but now that you're here, you'll stay in the house or..." His hands clenched and unclenched.

"Or what?" Jenny faced him. "Or you'll throw me on a camel and send me off into the desert?" She shook her head. "It's too late, Mike. I'm here and I'm staying. You know I have every confidence in you, in how you're running things. All I want to do is to get into the Hurani house and see for myself that Timmie's all right. I'll wear a robe and a veil. I'll be careful. I'll—"

"Do you know what they'll do to you if you're discovered?"

"I won't be discovered."

"If you're lucky," he went on as though he hadn't heard her, "you'll be turned over to the local police." He looked at the other men, and switching to Jahanian, said, "I don't know what the local jail is like, but if it's anything like the jails I've seen in some of the other Middle Eastern countries, it's not a place you'd want to spend your summer vacation."

"It's a hell hole," Yassir said. "Last year a man who worked for my father was caught stealing oranges in the marketplace. My father was very angry when he heard, and so he did not go immediately to try to get the man released. By the time he got there..." He turned to Kumar. "I hesitate to speak of such things in the American lady's presence."

"Tell her," Kumar ordered.

"The man had been badly beaten," Yassir said. "He lay in his own excrement in a cell barely big enough to hold a large dog. The four fingers of his right hand had been cut off."

"You would not be that lucky," Kumar said harshly. "You're a foreign woman, an infidel. Do you understand what they would do to you?"

Jenny hesitated. "I understand the danger," she said as calmly as she could. "But I can't believe Aiden would let that happen to me."

"He abused you," Mike said. "He kidnapped your son. What makes you think he would protect you?"

"We were married for six years. In the beginning, I think he loved me. We've had a child. I know he changed after his father and Mustafa came, but I honestly believe there's a part of him that still cares for me."

"Are you willing to bet your life on that?"

She felt strangely calm, in control. The agitation she had felt earlier faded and she was certain in the knowledge that what she wanted to do was the right, the only thing to do.

"I know the layout of the house," she said. "Aiden described it so often I felt like I could walk in and know exactly where each room was located. He even drew a diagram of it, showing me his room, the living room, the room where they had their meals."

"Seferina also knows the layout," Kumar said. "She can describe it to us."

"Not very well," Seferina said. "In truth, Prince Ben Ari, I am confined to the kitchen. In the two weeks I have been there I have rarely ventured into the rest of the house."

"The gate opens into the garden," Jenny said. "On both sides there are bedrooms. A sitting room opens off a corridor just opposite the front entrance of the garden. Next to it is the dining room, and next to that a room that is a combination library and office, where the family records are kept. The kitchen is on the other side of the dining room at the back of the house. There are five bedrooms—two open off the garden, three are in the back."

She closed her eyes, struggling to remember every detail. "The walls completely encircle the house. Besides the main entrance, there is a gate in the wall that only the family knows about."

"A gate?" Bouchaib, the gardener, shook his head. "I know nothing of a gate," he said.

"It's there," Jenny insisted. "Aiden told me it was." She looked at Bouchaib. "We could find it," she said. "And if I were inside, I could tell you when it would be safe to unlock the gate and let the others in."

"It's too risky," Mike said. "I won't allow it."

"Risky, yes." Kumar nodded agreement. "But it just might work. With Jenny inside we could—"

"Seferina's inside," Mike said. "She can do whatever Jenny can do."

"But she doesn't know the layout of the house," Kumar argued. "I know it could be dangerous, Mike, but when Jenny is robed and veiled, I doubt that her own mother would recognize her. With her there to tell us the movements of the men and where the boy is, it would make what we have to do that much easier."

"No! Absolutely not! I won't have her exposed to that kind of danger."

"Look," Jenny said, trying to be reasonable. "It will only be for a few days. I know I can get away with it for that long."

"I won't even discuss it. You're not going and that's it."

The others began a heated discussion. They raised their voices. Madih shook his fist at Abdur. Omar Ben Ismail jumped to his feet and waved his arms. Kumar spoke once, sharply, and they quieted down.

Abdur said, "It would help us if the woman was in the house. There are the two brothers, the old man and servants. It would even the odds if we knew their whereabouts when we attacked."

"The woman would be in terrible danger," Yassir said.

"But if she is willing…" Omar Ben Ismail lifted his shoulders in a shrug. "After all, it is her son. It's only right that she take some of the risk."

"I for one think she should do it." Madih stroked his beard. "As you say, it is her son. Why should she let us take all of the risks?"

"*You* take no risk," Abdur said angrily. "You will be safe in this house while the rest of us try to get the boy."

"I could lose everything," Madih whined. "I'm offering you shelter. I—"

"For a price!" Omar snapped. "Prince Kumar is paying you handsomely."

Jenny listened to the arguments. She caught most of what they were saying, enough to know that some of them were in favor of her going to the Hurani house. She knew that she could be of help, but that wasn't the only reason she wanted in. For the past six months Timmie had lived in a strange and foreign household, away from anything he had ever known before. Perhaps by now he had adjusted, and she hoped for his sake that he had. But she could only imagine how terrified he would be when a group of men he had never seen burst into the house and took him away. No matter how it went, it would be bad, but if she were there to reassure him, perhaps she could lessen his fear.

She listened to the men arguing, and knew she would not be deterred. With or without their approval, she was determined to get inside the Hurani house.

"That's enough," Kumar finally said. And when the other men had quieted, he turned to Mike. "I know how you feel about this, and I understand. I, too, am aware of the risk Jenny would be taking. But I can understand her wanting to help and I honestly believe she could. If she stayed out of the way and kept her eyes and ears open, it could be invaluable to us. She could pass on whatever she learns to Seferina, and Seferina in turn could pass it on to Bouchaib."

There was a moment of silence. Jenny held her breath. The others waited.

No, he wouldn't let her do this. If anything happened to her... Mike couldn't even allow himself to think about that. Jenny Cooper Hurani had come to mean more to him than he wanted to admit. He'd known a lot of women, more than his share. Great looking, sexy women. He wasn't sure why Jenny had gotten to him. She'd walked into his office in Vegas that day looking scared and sad, and there'd been something about her that had touched him. He'd taken her case. And he'd dragged her out on the desert to prove to her that she wasn't strong enough to be a part of the rescue attempt. He'd been determined to break her, to force her to surrender. But he hadn't broken her; she hadn't surrendered.

In her own way she was the strongest woman he'd ever known. And the softest. Making love with her had been the best experience he'd ever had, a sharing of emotions, of heart and mind as well as of body. It had renewed him, changed him. Maybe he hadn't yet sorted out all that he felt for Jenny, but he knew he would do everything in his power to keep her safe, that he would lay down his life for her if he had to.

In a voice made rough by all he was feeling, he said, "You hired me to do a job, Jenny. This is my show and I'm damn well going to run it."

"Listen," she said. "I—"

"No, I won't listen. You'll do what you're told." He turned to Madih. "Call your woman," he said. "I want Mrs. Hurani taken to her room and I want her locked in. Do you understand?"

"Yes, *sidi.* Of course, *sidi.*" Madih sent Jenny a sly look, as though to say, "You see? This is the way women should be treated."

The look snapped something inside her and she turned on Mike, so furious she could barely speak. "I won't be treated like this," she said. "You can't keep me locked up."

"I can do anything I damn well want to do." His eyes were like cold steel. "When I agreed that you could come along, you told me that you'd follow or-

ders. So now I'm ordering you to stay here and I'm
having you locked up to make sure you do."

"You can't do this to me."

"Oh, yes, I can."

Tears of anger and humiliation rose in her eyes. "I'll
never forgive you for this," she whispered.

That almost got to him. He wanted to pull her into
his arms, to tell her that he was doing it because he
cared about her, because the idea of losing her chilled
his very soul. But he wouldn't soften, wouldn't re-
lent.

Fatima came in. Madih barked an order. The
woman motioned to Jenny. Jenny looked at Kumar
for support, but he only shook his head and said,
"Mike is running the show, Jenny. I'm sorry."

Yassir mumbled something, then, getting to his feet,
said to Mike, "It is not right you treat a woman in this
manner. You should not lock her in her room. You
should not do this."

"Leave it alone." Kumar put a restraining hand on
Yassir's arm. "Do not overstep, my friend."

Madih said, "Take her," and with a murmured
apology, Fatima took her arm and led her out of the
room.

Jenny looked back at Mike, still unable to believe
that he would do this to her. He met her gaze, but only
for a moment. Then he looked away.

Never, for as long as he lived, would he forget the
way Jenny had looked at him. Don't you know, he'd
wanted to say, can't you see it's because I care about
you? Because if anything happened to you I'd never
forgive myself? You hired me to get your son back to
you, but when I made the commitment to take the job,

I also made the commitment to myself that I would protect you.

And he would, even if it meant losing her.

God, how he admired her courage. Even in the presence of the men, the sneering look on Youssef Madih's face, his own anger, she had not backed down.

He paced the length of the small, scraggly garden. She hated him now and he didn't blame her. In time she would understand that he was right. Maybe she'd even forgive him for his harsh words. But in the meantime?

He couldn't leave it like this between them. He had to do something about it.

A sound awakened her. She lay still for a moment, waiting, listening. From the dim light that came in the narrow window she saw the doorknob turn. Scarcely daring to breathe, she sat up and reached toward the chair for the gun.

The door squeaked open. She leveled the gun.

"Jenny?" The voice was a whisper in the darkness. "Jenny?"

"What do you want?" she asked.

Mike closed the door behind him and came into the room. "To talk to you."

"Get out."

"Not until we talk about this." He took the gun out of her hand and sat on the edge of the bed beside her. "I hurt your feelings before. I'm sorry."

"Are you?" Jenny glared at him. "How dare you send me away like that? How dare you have me locked in this room?"

"I dared because I care about you. Because I've got you in my blood and in my bones and my brain, and because the thought of anything happening to you makes me crazy." He gripped her shoulders. "Don't you know the way I feel about you, Jenny? Can't you understand that I'm trying to protect you?"

"And can't you understand that I'm trying to protect my son?" She wanted so desperately for him to know how she felt, to convince him that the love and concern she had for her son made her willing to brave any danger, face any foe. "I know I can help," she said. "If you'll only let me."

"No," he said sharply. "No."

"Mike, please . . ."

He pulled her closer and stopped her words with a kiss. She tried to protest, and when she did, his arms tightened around her. "Jenny," he said against her lips. "Jenny."

She told herself that this didn't solve anything, but her lips parted under his and her arms crept up to hold him as he held her. Hunger replaced anger; the need to be with him was too strong to be denied.

When he eased her back against the bed, she didn't protest. He lay down beside her and held her so close against him she could feel the wild thumping of his heart. She made herself say, "We have to talk. We have to—"

He took her words and kissed her with all of the pent-up emotion he'd tried to hold in check. She was his now and he wouldn't let her go.

And when she said, "Darling...oh, darling...." he felt all the anger and pain he'd ever known soften and crumble.

She sighed against him and opened his shirt so that she could feel his skin against her breasts. "It's been so long," she said.

"Too long."

He rolled away from her to kick off his sandals and remove his trousers. Then he was beside her, holding her. He took her mouth and whispered, "Touch me," and her body went weak with desire.

He kissed her breasts and touched her as she touched him. He felt her heated moistness and grew hard and rigid in her hand. And at last, when it was past bearing, he came over her and into her and they began to move as one.

"So good," he murmured against her lips. "Ah, Jenny. Sweet Jenny-girl."

He moved slowly against her, his body lean and hard, covering hers, holding her as she held him. He took her mouth. He touched her breasts, and squeezed the aching nipples between his fingertips.

She loved it. Loved the feel of him over her, inside her. Loved his kiss, his touch, his scent, the feel of his skin against hers.

And him. For now she knew it was true: she could not be like this with him if there was not love. And it seemed to her, even as they moved so wildly, so hotly against one another, that she had known it from the very beginning, from that last night on the desert in Death Valley when they had looked at each other across the camp fire. He had kissed her that night and she had known that at that moment, love had begun.

Love. She wanted to tell him, but because she could not, she lifted her body to his and held him close. And tried to say with her touch what she could not say with words.

He tightened his arms around her. He cupped her bottom and rocked her closer. He thrust hard and deep, and she turned her head into his shoulder to smother her cry of pleasure.

"My Jenny," he whispered. "My Jenny."

It was too perfect to last, and clinging to him, she began the climb toward that ultimate moment, somewhere between agony and ecstasy, striving, striving…and then it came, glorious, heart-stopping. Her body soared, met his, and together they tumbled off the edge of forever.

He held her and caressed her. He smoothed the damp curls back off her face and kissed her trembling lips. He said, "Forgive me for before. If I hurt you, if I made you angry, it's because I care about you. Because I'm afraid for you. I only want to keep you safe, Jenny. Believe that."

"I do," she said.

He brushed a kiss across her eyes. "Go to sleep. We'll talk again in the morning."

"I wish you could stay with me."

"So do I." He let her go and sat up. "But it wouldn't look good, especially for you."

"I know."

He sat on the edge of the bed and pulled his clothes on. "I'll see you in the morning," he said. "We'll talk then." He kissed her and turned away. But at the door he hesitated. "I'm sorry this was locked before. I won't lock it when I leave."

Jenny held her arms out to him. "One more kiss," she said.

He came back and kissed her, then straightened and went quickly out the door.

She lay where she was, looking up at the ceiling. And knew what she had to do.

Chapter 11

In the first faint light of dawn, Jenny got up and dressed in the black robe and veil, the wig, and the scarf that covered it. Because the small bag that held her clothes had an American label, she bundled the few things she would take with her in the extra head scarf: a change of clothing, the orange giraffe and the envelope of photographs.

She had no plan; she only knew that somehow she had to find the Hurani house, and that once she did, she would appeal to Seferina to take her in.

The corridor outside her room was empty. She followed it to the patio. There were no sounds, not even the barking of a dog. She looked around, then moved quietly out and headed for the gate at the far end. She was almost across it when she heard a snick of a sound.

"Who's there?" The voice, low and deadly, was only a few feet away.

She sank back into the shadow of a date palm.

"*Balak!* Move out!"

She took a step backward.

"*Baraka!* Stop, or I will shoot!"

"Wait," Jenny whispered in English, all of the Jahanian she'd learned forgotten in the moment of fear. "Don't—don't shoot."

"Come forward where I can see you."

She did as she was commanded and saw young Yassir, his rifle aimed and ready. She froze. "It is I. Me. Jenny. Jenny Hurani," she managed to say.

"Madame Hurani? What are you doing outside? Where are you...?" He saw the bundle of clothes wrapped in the scarf. "You are leaving?" He shook his head. "But you cannot. You must return to your room at once. You are bidden to stay here."

"Yassir, please..." She searched for the words that would convince him to let her go. And though very likely it was *haram* to touch a man you were not married or betrothed to, she took his arm and drew him back into the shadow of the pepper trees. As she did, ducking her head to escape the low-hanging branches, her veil caught and fell from her face.

Yassir quickly retrieved it and handed it to her. He had meant, as was only right, to avert his eyes, but because he was curious to see the face of this American woman whose hair was the color of sunlight, he allowed himself one quick glance. And could not look away.

"Ay," he whispered. "Ay, *madame*. You are beautiful. So beautiful."

Jenny started to turn away and fasten the veil over her face, but instead she hesitated. Use whatever advantage you have, a voice inside her head whispered.

You have to get to Timmie. Any way you can. She looked up at Yassir. His expression was awestruck, his dark eyes soft with wonder and desire.

She touched his arm again. "Please help me," she said in a voice that trembled with all that she was feeling. "I haven't seen my little boy in over six months. He's all I have, Yassir. My heart aches for him. I know that you and Prince Kumar and the others are strong and capable men and that I am only a woman and weak. But I have knowledge of the Hurani house. If I can get in, if Seferina will help me, then I can help you."

Tears that were not completely theatrical filled Jenny's eyes. "Let me go," she pleaded. "Please, I beg of you."

"Do not cry, *madame*." He clutched her hand and brought it to his lips. "I cannot bear to see your pain."

"Then help me, Yassir. Please help me."

"If you are caught…" A shudder ran through him. "You do not know what they would do to you," he whispered.

"It will only be for a day or two. I'll stay out of sight. I'll be all right until you and the others come."

She raised her face; her eyes were shining with tears. And he was lost.

He touched her hair. "I should not," he said, as though to himself.

"Please," she whispered.

"I will take you," he said.

Her heart leapt. She needed his help; she had no idea how to get to the Huranis on her own. But what if Yassir got into trouble because of her? What happened to a young man who disobeyed orders? No, she told herself. This wasn't the army. Surely Kumar, if he discovered that Yassir had helped her, would not punish him.

The hour was early. There would be less suspicion if she were with a man rather than being on the street alone. She put her doubts aside and said, "Thank you, Yassir. I will never forget your kindness."

"Come," he told her. "Put on your veil. We must slip away before anyone discovers you are gone."

They crossed the patio, and when he had opened the gate, they went out into the street. "It is almost six kilometers," he said. "We must hurry before day comes and there are people about."

Except for a dog or two, the street was deserted. They didn't speak as they hurried along, past the dye works of Madih, past small dwellings, another mosque, a blacksmith. There were few houses this far from the center of town, more trees here, a thin stream where tethered camels could drink. Finally ahead she saw a gray stone wall and the house beyond.

"The house of Hurani," Yassir said.

Jenny's mouth was dry, the palms of her hands suddenly damp.

"We will go in and around to the back where the kitchen is." He took her arm. "There will be a guard, but I will tell him you are Seferina's cousin, come from a neighboring town. Keep your head lowered and do not speak."

They approached the gate. A man appeared.

"Who are you?" he challenged. "What do you want here?"

"I am bringing the cousin of Seferina, the cook. She is to work in the kitchen."

"No one told me a servant was coming today."

Yassir stiffened. His voice grew harsh. "Do you want to wake the master of the house at this hour to verify what I say? Where is the bell? I myself will call for him."

"No, no, that is not necessary. I believe you." The man grunted and rubbed his eyes. "The woman Seferina complains all the time of too much work." He peered at Jenny, but she kept her head down. "All right," he said. "You may go."

"How do we find the kitchen?"

"Go around the garden to the back of the house. Even now Seferina must be preparing breakfast. No doubt she will be glad for the help."

"*Shukran,*" Yassir bowed. "Come, woman," he said to Jenny, and leaving her to follow behind, headed for the house.

It was bigger than Youssef Madih's, of one story, low and rambling. Somewhere inside was her son. And Aiden, his father and Mustafa. Her heart beat so hard she was sure Yassir could hear it. Fear mingled with excitement, and the knowledge that at last she was close to her little boy.

They entered a courtyard. Goats nibbled spiky weeds. A donkey was tied to the trunk of a palm. There were several doors. One was open. They could hear the rattle of pots and pans.

"Come," Yassir said.

Jenny tightened her hands together in the folds of her robe.

He went ahead of her, into the kitchen. Seferina was at the stove. "*Sabbah al khair,*" he said in greeting.

She turned, surprised. "Yassir?" she said. "Is that you? What are you doing here so early in the morning?"

"I have brought your cousin from Taboku," he said.

"What? What are you talking about? I have no cousin in Taboku. I..." She turned to Jenny, her eyes wide with shock. *"Zfft!"* she exclaimed, and with a glance over her shoulder, closed the door that led into the rest of the house. "Are you mad?" she whispered when she turned back to them. "It was decided that she not come. You must take her back immediately."

"Please," Jenny said in a whisper. "I'm here now. You must let me stay."

"It is madness. If you are discovered—"

"I won't be, but if I am, I'll say that I fooled you, that you did not know who I was. You had asked in the marketplace if anyone knew of a kitchen helper, and when I appeared, you thought someone had sent me. Tell them I pretended to be a simpleminded girl and that you didn't have the heart to send me away."

"No," Seferina said angrily. "I will not! You must go."

But Jenny shook her head. "I'm here and this is where I will stay until I have my son." Her voice was firm, not to be argued with. "You can't make me go, Seferina, so accept the fact that I am here."

The woman looked from Jenny to Yassir. "She will stay," he said. "That's an order."

"Zfft!" Seferina said again. Then with a curt nod to Yassir, she muttered, "You had better go. It is best they do not see you here."

He looked at Jenny.

"I'll be all right," she said.

"Inshallah," he whispered. "It is the will of God that all will go well with you."

"Shukran, Yassir. I'll never forget your kindness."

"*Madame...*" He shook his head, then quickly turned and hurried out the door.

And Jenny was alone with Seferina. Here in the house of Hurani.

Mike was asleep when Kumar pounded on the door of his room. "What...?" he muttered. "What is it? Who's there?"

Kumar came in. "She's gone!" he cried. "Jenny's gone!"

Mike sat up and rubbed his eyes. "What're you talking about?"

"Jenny's not in her room. Her door was locked. How did she get out?"

Brennan sucked in his breath, then, with a muttered curse, threw back the sheet. "Are you sure? Have you checked the house?"

"Every inch. The patio, the courtyard. She isn't here." He glared at Brennan. "How did she get out of her room?"

Mike looked up at his friend, then away. "She got out because I'm a damn fool," he wanted to say. "Because making love with her weakened my knees and addled my brain. Because I trusted her."

"It's my fault," he said. "I went to—to see her last night. I didn't lock her door when I left."

"You made love to her," Kumar accused.

"Yeah." Brennan shook his head. "That's why I didn't lock her in afterward. It would have seemed..." He shrugged. "Hell, Kumar, I can't explain it. It would have seemed like I was taking advantage of her, making love, leaving..." He ran a hand through his hair. "I couldn't do it," he said.

Kumar's face clouded with anger. "So much for that strictly professional relationship," he growled. "She has gone to the Hurani house, of course."

"Of course." Mike's stomach knotted with fear. He thought of the French woman journalist who had been beaten and raped. And of the woman who had been stoned. The American paper had described the second incident in chilling detail. The men had surrounded her. They had picked up stones, small ones at first, and hurled them at her. Then bigger and still bigger stones, making it last, beating her down, breaking her bones, punishing her for her sins before finally the large rocks were hurled and she lay bloody and dead at their feet.

He crushed his fist against his mouth so that he wouldn't cry out.

"Take it easy, my friend," Kumar said in a quiet voice. "She is there now and there is little we can do. If she can remain undiscovered for the next two or three days there is hope that we will get both her and the boy out safely." He rested a hand on Mike's shoulder. "Get dressed. The men are waiting. We will discuss how best to proceed. Allah is good; he will not let us fail."

"Inshallah," Mike murmured. *"Inshallah.* If Allah wills."

When Kumar left, he went into the small stall shower. Jenny was gone. She was inside the Hurani household. If they discovered her there... He moaned aloud and struck the wall with his fist. "God," he said aloud. "God help her."

And it was then he knew how much he loved her.

* * *

They were waiting for him when he went into the other room. Kumar's face was grim, angry. Abdur stroked his worry beads and did not look up. Madih said, "The punishment will be severe."

"I know what I did was wrong," Mike said. "I—"

Kumar stopped him. "We are speaking of Yassir."

"Yassir? What has Yassir to do with this?"

"He helped the woman to escape," Madih spat. "Because of him we will all be killed. It is his fault. I'll kill him with my own hands." He started toward Yassir, who stood, arms at his sides, head bowed.

"Stop." Kumar put out a detaining hand. "Sit down, Madih." He turned to Yassir. "Tell us what happened," he said. "You were on guard. How did the woman slip past you?"

"She did not slip past, Prince Kumar. I let her go. I accompanied her to the Hurani house."

"Son of a..." Mike pushed Kumar aside and grabbed young Yassir by the neck of his robe. "You what?" he roared.

Yassir didn't flinch. "I found her in the patio. I was going to stop her but—" He shook his head. "—but I could not. She pleaded with me. I understood her need to be with her son." He looked Mike in the eye. "I helped her, *sidi,* and I would do it again if she asked. I would lay down my life for her if she asked me to do it."

Mike's anger faded as quickly as it had come. He understood. Yassir, too, had fallen under Jenny's spell. He, too, had fallen in love with her. And because he had, he'd risked the wrath and the possible punishment of his colleagues to help her.

How can I be angry with him? Mike asked himself. I know how he feels. I, too, would lay down my life for her.

He let Yassir go. "It's done," he said.

"You do not blame me, Mr. Brennan? You do not wish to have me punished?"

"No, Yassir, I don't blame you, nor do I want to see you punished." Mike turned to the others. "All right," he said, "let's decide where we go from here."

They gathered around the table. Fatima brought hot mint tea and flat bread. As soon as she left, Kumar said, "We can be ready to go in the day after tomorrow."

Mike, his fists clenched, looked around the circle of men. Three days. Could she hold out that long?

The morning passed. Jenny helped Seferina prepare the breakfast. When the manservant came to take it to the dining room to serve, he looked at Jenny in surprise.

"Who is this?" he asked.

"My cousin from Taboku. She has come to help me." Seferina gave him an angry look. "I cannot do all this work alone. All I do is slave from sunup to sundown. The only time I get out is to buy more food." She banged a pan. "No wonder the other cook left so suddenly. How can one woman be expected to cook for such a large household?"

"All right! All right!" The man held his hands up in front of him as though to ward off a blow. Muttering under his breath, he took the tray of food and left the kitchen.

"*Shukran,*" Jenny said. "Thank you."

"I do not do it for you. If you are discovered I will be as guilty as you. They will kill me for betraying the house of Hurani."

"But surely the law would not allow that to happen."

"The law? The only law in Al Hamaan is the law of Mustafa Hurani."

Mustafa. A chill of fear ran down Jenny's spine, and something else: suddenly she felt suffused with guilt. She had risked everything in her need to rescue her son. But was it right to risk other people's lives: Seferina, young Yassir? Kumar and his men? Mike?

She thought of how he must have felt this morning when he discovered she had gone. He had trusted her and she had betrayed that trust.

But I'm here now, she told herself. Later—if there is a later—I'll make him see that I had to do this. I couldn't stand by and do nothing. I have to be here for Tim.

In spite of her worries, the morning passed quickly. As soon as breakfast had been completed it was time to prepare lunch.

"Eat, eat, eat," Seferina complained. "That's all they do in this house. I work from morning till night preparing food." She took a *tahine*, a cone-lidded, earthenware pot, from one of the shelves and began to chop vegetables into it, muttering all the while. She picked up the pierced *kuskus* steamer and asked Jenny if she knew how to prepare the dish.

"Yes," Jenny said, and reached for the semolina.

"We will also have *mahshi kusah*." Seferina dumped a bag of zucchini into the sink and began to scrub them. When that was done she fried ground meat and added the spices and pine nuts she had prepared earlier.

"So many things?" Jenny asked.

Seferina nodded. "Every day it is the same. I cook, they eat. I took this job because Prince Kumar asked me to, because he wanted someone he could trust inside the house." She looked up from the zucchinis. "I do not think I have been of much help. The Hurani men are suspicious of everything and everybody. The boy is watched. If he goes into the courtyard, his father or his uncle are with him."

"And at night?" Jenny paused in what she was doing. "Is he guarded at night?"

Seferina shook her head. "One of the servants told me that he was when he first came, but not now."

"Where is his room?"

"It is next to his father's. Down the hall..." She paused and with a frown said, "Do not even think of going to his room, *madame.*"

"I just want to know where it is," Jenny said. "When Mike and Kumar come I want to be able to get to Timmie as quickly as I can."

"Very well, I will tell you. The boy's room is at the end of the corridor. His father's room is next to it."

"And Mustafa's room?"

"Across from the boy's."

So Timmie was virtually surrounded—his father next to him, Mustafa across the hall. That frightened her, because she knew it would be difficult to get to him without being detected. And because she knew she had to try.

"Where will I sleep?" she asked.

"In my room, to the left of the kitchen. There is only a single bed, so you will have to sleep on the floor. I'll ask one of the servants for a blanket for you to sleep on.''

"What time do the men retire?"

"You ask a lot of questions."

"I need a lot of answers." Jenny's expression was serious, commanding. "I need to know everything I can about the house," she said sternly. "I want to know the routine, when and if the men ever leave and how long they're gone." She looked for a piece of paper, and when she didn't see one, asked, "Do you have paper and pencil?"

"Why?"

"Do you?"

Seferina frowned. Then she opened a drawer and handed Jenny the stub of a pencil.

And when Jenny said, "Paper?" Seferina searched through the drawer until she found a piece.

Jenny smoothed it out. "All right," she said, "I'm going to draw a sketch of the house from what I remember, but you'll have to help me. We're here." She indicated the kitchen. "The dining room opens off the kitchen, doesn't it?"

And when Seferina said that it did, Jenny began to draw a diagram of the house from what she remembered Aiden telling her. Though Seferina complained that she knew little, Jenny kept after her, asking if one room opened off the other, which rooms opened into the courtyard, if there were windows big enough for a man to crawl through.

When she finished, she had a pretty fair idea of where every room in the house was located. Now she would need to ask Bouchaib, the gardener, about the gate that Aiden had once told her opened off the patio.

He came into the kitchen an hour later. Though obviously shocked to find Jenny there, he had little to say—until she mentioned, "I want to go outside and look for the gate that Aiden told me about. Will you take me?"

"There is no gate."

"Yes, there is." She put down the knife she had been using, gathered up potato skins and put them in a clay bowl. "If someone asks, you can say we're feeding the goats." Her voice brooked no argument. She went to the door. "Come along," she said. "This is something the others will need to know."

He grumbled, but he came. And when they were in the yard, he said, "There is no gate except for the main entrance. If there was a gate I, Bouchaib al Shaibi, would know of it."

Jenny paid no attention as she moved farther back in the garden, where trees and vines grew thickly. She started at one end of the wall, Bouchaib behind her, and fought her way through the tangle of under-brush.

The wall was old, the stones crumbling. She saw no sign of an entrance, but she went on, sure of what Aiden had told her. Bouchaib followed behind her, mumbling and complaining that there was no gate. She paid no attention as she pushed her way through the tangled vines, because she knew there had to be a secret opening in the wall. And at last she saw it. The mortar had crumbled, the climbing vines had hidden it, but it was there. And it was unlocked.

"Tonight you will go to the house of Youssef Madih and tell the others about the gate. Do you understand?"

"I do not like a woman giving me orders."

"You will do as I say," Jenny insisted. "Because if you do not, I will tell Prince Kumar that you refused to help when help was needed." She took a step closer. "You will go at dark tonight. You will leave Prince Kumar this sketch of the house that I have made and you will explain how he and his men are to enter through this gate. Then you will return, and in the morning tell me when they will come."

She didn't like giving orders, but she would have stood up to the devil himself if it meant helping Timmie.

Bouchaib mumbled something else, then, head lowered, said, "Very well. I will go to the house of Madih tonight." And with that he turned and walked away from her.

She went back through the tangle of garden to where the goats were, gave them the potato peelings, then returned to the kitchen.

Where Mustafa Hurani waited.

She faltered in the doorway. Seferina shot her a terrified look. Mustafa, thick arms crossed over his chest, frowned at her.

Jenny cast her eyes down. "I fed the goats like you told me, Cousin," she murmured in a slow and stumbling voice. "What would you like me to do now?"

For a moment Seferina couldn't answer. Then she said, "Scrub the floor, girl. Do not stand there like the dummy you are, get busy!"

"Who is she?" Mustafa demanded. "Who told you to hire her? We're not made of money. We won't pay another girl."

"She works for no pay," Seferina said. "Only for what scraps of food I will give her. And she will sleep on the floor of my room. She will cost you nothing. You will not even know that she is here."

Jenny kept her head lowered.

"Well..." Mustafa stroked his mustache.

"I have much work," Seferina whined. "I need help, *sidi.* I'm an old woman—I can't do everything myself. I—"

"Keep her then, but out of the way."

"I will, *sidi.*"

"Where are you from, girl?" he asked.

"Ta-Taboku," Jenny whispered. And hid her trembling hands in the folds of her robe.

"She is not to go into the other part of the house," Mustafa said.

"No, *sidi.*"

"We will eat soon?"

"In an hour."

"Hurry it up then." He turned to leave, but at the door he hesitated. "There is something about you, girl. Have I ever seen you before?"

Jenny thought her heart would stop. "No, *sidi,*" she managed to say.

He rubbed a hand across his face. "Strange," he mumbled. "Strange."

When he was gone, she and Seferina looked at each other.

"You must be careful," Seferina whispered.

Jenny clutched the edge of the sink for support. "I know," she said.

Chapter 12

Seferina snored, earth-shattering, wall-shaking surges of sound interspersed with snorts and rattles and gut-deep moans. There was no escape. The noise filled the room, making sleep impossible.

The blanket Jenny lay upon was thin; the floor was hard. She twisted and turned, unable to find a comfortable position, and covered her ears in an effort to blot out the terrible rumbles from the bed only a few feet away. At last she got up, put her robe on and slipped out the door into the yard.

The goats moved restlessly, the donkey brayed. But the animals' noise was nothing compared to Seferina's snoring. Jenny moved farther into the garden, staying close to the shadow of the trees. Then she stopped and looked back at the house.

Timmie slept in one of the rooms there, and she tried to picture him, curled up in his bed, small fist against his cheek. What dreams did he dream? What images of the home he'd been taken away from stirred his unconscious? Did he think of her? Remember her?

Tears stung Jenny's eyes. It was a special kind of torture to be so close and not to be able to go to him. If only she could see him, even for a moment, it would ease the ache in her heart.

She told herself she had to be patient. A mistake now could ruin everything. But there was in her that mother instinct that would not be denied. Timmie was here; she had to see him.

She went back into the house and slipped from the bedroom into the kitchen, then to the dining room. Her feet were bare, and she moved without a sound into the hall. A floorboard creaked and she stopped, scarcely daring to breathe. When there was no other sound, she crept slowly forward—tense, throat dry, stomach in knots, but compelled by a force greater than common sense or fear to go on.

Past Aiden's room. Don't think about that, she told herself. You're almost there.

Slowly, quietly, she moved on tiptoes through the darkness. The room across the hall was Mustafa's. If he was awake, if he heard her... If he found her... Her heart thudded hard against her ribs and she hesitated. Should she go back? Should she go on? But she was close now, so close to her little son. A few steps more.

She turned the doorknob of his room and took a step inside. The window curtain moved in the slight breeze off the desert. By the moon-cast shadows she saw a dresser. A bed. She went forward, holding her breath, and stood at the side of the bed.

Timmie was curled on his side, his hand curved against his cheek just as she had imagined. Her baby, her little boy.

Silent tears ran down her cheeks and she had to clench her hands to her sides to keep from touching him. He wore a rough cotton nightgown that covered him from his neck to his feet.

How she yearned to touch his soft cheek—just one touch, one small embrace. To gather him in her arms, to whisper, "Mama's here, Timmie. Mama's come to take you home."

But she did not. She only stood looking down at him, crying her silent tears.

Mike paced up and down in his room. He couldn't sleep. Every time he closed his eyes he saw images of her in his mind: the way she had looked that night in Death Valley when she'd come up out of the pool and into his arms. He remembered every whisper, every sigh of every time they had made love.

He thought of her bravery, her courage, her stamina in the cruel desert heat. He saw again the determined expression on her face when she'd followed him up one sand dune and down another, sweating, swearing under her breath, but not giving up, never giving up.

Here in Jahan she had stood up to him and the other men. With a warning flash of her dove gray eyes and a stubborn thrust of her small chin she had faced prejudice and the centuries-old Arabian-style machismo. In spite of all odds, against masculine opposition, she had been determined to do whatever had to be done to get her son back.

She had walked fearlessly into the terrible danger of the Hurani household, and while he wanted to wring Yassir's neck, he didn't altogether blame the younger man. Jenny was an appealing woman. If she turned on the charm, he doubted there was a man of any age or race who'd be able to resist her.

She was strong and she was beautiful. But he knew deep in his gut that this time she had made a mistake. She had let her love for her son overrule her reason; she'd underestimated the danger.

She had said that she did not believe her ex-husband would harm her, but how could she be sure? Even if Aiden Hurani wanted to protect her, there would still be his father and his brother to deal with. From what Jenny had told him of Aiden's brother, he had a feeling that Mustafa Hurani would stop at nothing to protect the honor of the household. Jenny was a foreigner, a woman, an infidel. If he caught her he would squash her like a bug.

But until he and Kumar and the other men attacked there was nothing Mike could do. He could only hope and pray that she would be careful. That she would not get caught.

Jenny and Seferina had finished cleaning up from breakfast and had already started on the midday meal when the man who served came in.

"Old Tamar is sending me on an errand today," he told Seferina. "He needs more men in the oil fields. I am to get them and bring them here. Therefore, I will not be here to serve at the next meal. The new woman will serve in my place."

Seferina stopped what she was doing. She did not look at Jenny when she said, "I am more accustomed to the ways of the house. It is best that I serve."

"No!" he said sharply. "My lord Mustafa told me that she will do it, therefore she will." He looked suspiciously from Seferina to Jenny, who stood with her back to him near the sink. "Is there a reason why she cannot? Is she so addlepated she cannot do a simple thing like serve a meal? If she is, then she should not be here, because she is of no use."

"All right, all right." Seferina threw her hands into the air. "She will serve, but do not blame me if she makes a mess of it."

"She'd better not. The old man can be difficult, but Mustafa..." The servant shook his head. "He will box her ears and send her away if she makes a mistake." He glared at Seferina. "See that she does not."

When he left, the two women looked at each other. "You could leave now," Seferina said. "I will tell them you were frightened about serving and that you fled before I could stop you."

Jenny shook her head, for though the idea of being in the same room with Aiden and his father and brother terrified her, she was determined that she would not leave. Tomorrow Mike and Kumar would come. If there was fighting, gunfire and frightening shouts she had to be here for Timmie.

"It will be all right," she said to Seferina. "You'll tell me exactly what to do and I'll do it."

"If they should recognize you..." The woman shook her head. "It is too dangerous," she muttered. "For all of us."

"I'll keep my head lowered. I won't speak unless I'm spoken to. They won't expect me to carry on a conversation."

"They will kill you. They will kill me."

Jenny went to the older woman and put an hand on her shoulder. "No, they won't," she said softly. "Because they're not going to know who I am. I am your cousin from Taboku, a simple girl who has come to help in the kitchen. It will be all right. I won't give myself away."

The words were said with confidence, as much for Seferina's sake as for her own. She must not let Seferina know how frightened she was at the thought of being in the same room with the man she had lived with for six years. Her body was covered by a robe, her face hidden behind a veil. But what if Aiden looked into her eyes? Would he know her then? Would Mustafa? And if they did...

The plate she had been drying slipped from her hands and fell to the floor, where it broke.

"So you are afraid," Seferina said in a low voice.

"No... No, I—I wasn't paying attention to what I was doing, that's all."

But she had lied. She was afraid.

The midday meal was served at two. The three men were seated on the floor around a low table that she had set before they'd come in. On it Jenny had already placed the *mazzah*, the Middle Eastern hors d'oeuvres. There were slices of ripe cantaloupe, feta cheese, a dish of black olives, and herb-stuffed sardines that had been grilled in vine leaves.

When it was time to go in again, she stood behind the door leading into the dining room, then, with head bowed, she entered, carrying a steaming dish of lamb stew with rice.

The men looked up and gave her a cursory glance. "Where is Abdul?" Aiden asked.

"I sent him to J'dirya," his father said.

"This is the new girl." Mustafa wiped his mouth with the back of his hand. "She is the cousin of Seferina, from Taboku."

"What is your name, girl?" Aiden asked.

Name? It hadn't occurred to her that she would need one. Her mind went blank. She couldn't think of a single Arabian woman's name.

"Well?" Tamar sounded impatient. "Speak up! Speak up!"

His wife's name—she remembered that. "Zahira," she said. "Zahira, *sidi.*"

"Blasphemy!" Tamar said with a laugh. "Sheer blasphemy that such an ignorant girl would have the same name as my beloved wife, may Allah rest her soul. There is not a day that goes by that I do not think of her. She was the perfect woman, the model wife. Loyal, subservient, the mother of my sons."

Another door opened and the old man looked up. "Here you are at last," he said to the little boy standing in the doorway.

For a moment Jenny couldn't breathe. She could only look at her son. He wore a white robe. He was taller by at least two inches than he had been seven months ago. His hair had been dyed a dull black, but the cowlick that had refused to curl was still there, a small patch of hair standing at attention at the crown of his head.

"Come and sit down next to me," Aiden said. "Let me give you a sardine." He put one of the stuffed sardines on a plate with a piece of feta cheese and a few olives and handed it to the boy.

"I like these little fishes," Timmie said in English.

But before he could pick one up, Mustafa reached across the table and slapped the boy's hand. "Speak Jahanian," he said in a loud voice. "You're not in America now. You are here and this is where you will stay. And you will, by Allah, speak the language." He slapped the boy again. "Remember or be punished."

It took every bit of Jenny's self-control not to cry out. She had actually raised the steaming hot dish to pour it over Mustafa's head when she stopped herself. With hands that trembled with the need to strike out, she made herself place the dish in the center of the table.

"I do not like it when you strike the boy," Aiden said. "He is my son. I will discipline him when it is necessary."

"You? Ha! You are as easy on him as you were with your infidel wife. You forget that he has her blood as well as yours and that you must do everything you can to wipe away all memory of that time in his life. He is Jahanian. One day he will rule the house of Hurani. If you allow him to be a weak boy he will grow to be a weak man." He turned to Timmie. "Ask for your food properly and it will be given to you."

Timmie's mouth trembled. "I don't remember," he whispered.

"Then you cannot have it." Mustafa pointed to the lamb dish. "What is this?" he asked.

"*Ka...*" Timmie hesitated. "*Kabsah,*" he said. "But I don't like it."

"Then you will eat nothing," Mustafa said. "You will sit here until we finish and then you will go to your room."

"But I'm hungry," Timmie whispered.

And because she could not help herself, Jenny said, in her slow and careful Jahanian, "There is also *lahm m'ajun.* Perhaps you would like some of that."

Timmie looked up at her. "It's almost like pizza, isn't it?" He smiled. "Yes, I like that."

"Then bring it for the boy," Aiden said without looking at her.

"You spoil him." Mustafa frowned. And to Jenny he said, "After this you will speak when you are spoken to, girl. Now be silent and fetch the rest of the food. I want no further disturbance at this table."

Jenny clenched her teeth. She'd never wanted to hit anyone before, but oh, God, how she ached to strike out at this man who had struck her child.

Tight-lipped, she turned away, but before she could move, Mustafa grabbed her arm. "Wait," he said.

Terror replaced anger. She raised her head, but only slightly.

"When I speak to you, you say, 'Yes, *sidi*,' or 'No, *sidi*.' Do you understand?"

She lowered her head. "Yes, *sidi*."

His grip on her arm tightened. "Have I seen you before?"

"In the kitchen, *sidi*."

"No." He shook his head. "Somewhere else." He released her. "You're from where?"

"The village of Taboku, *sidi*."

"I have never been there, but I know I have seen you. It will come to me. Now go and bring the rest of the food."

"Yes, *sidi*."

On legs that felt like limp, wet noodles, Jenny went out of the dining room. Once in the kitchen, she staggered to the sink. Head down, she took several deep breaths, then turned on the water and splashed her face.

"Are you all right?" Seferina asked, her own face gone pale with fear. "Did it go badly? Did they recognize you?"

"No." Jenny put the palms of her wet hands on her hot cheeks. "No, I don't think so. But Mustafa..." She took another deep breath. "He's a terrible man, Seferina. He slapped my little boy. It was all I could do not to hit him. I wanted to pour the lamb over his head."

She had a sudden vision of Mustafa with lamb stew running over his head and down his face and laughed. She clamped a hand over her mouth to muffle the sound. The laughter had the edge of hysteria to it. Before she could stop herself, it turned to tears. She brushed them away and fought for control.

"I have to go back," she told Seferina. "I said I would bring the *lahm m'ajun*."

"Are you sure you're all right?"

Jenny nodded.

"Then here." Seferina handed her the pizzalike dish, along with a plate of baklava. "Take these in and come back immediately. Do not speak."

Jenny didn't. She served the two dishes and, though it was difficult, kept her eyes averted. When she had finished serving, she turned away and went to the door leading to the kitchen. But there she hesitated and looked back for one more glimpse of her son. Soon, she silently told him. Soon we'll be together.

Then, as though drawn by some evil force to his gaze, she saw Mustafa watching her. In his eyes was a look of speculation that sent a chill of sheer terror down her spine.

"We go in tomorrow at midnight," Mike said to Bouchaib. "You're certain about the gate in the wall?"

"Yes, *sidi*. The woman found it just as she said she would. It is not locked. I will wait for you there. She also gave me the diagram of the house to give to you. On the night you come, the door to the kitchen will be open. You can go in through there." He twisted his worry beads. "I hope all will go well," he said. "That there will be little fighting."

"We hope so, too." Kumar patted Bouchaib on his shoulder. "There are only three of them," he said. "We expect no problem."

"I have heard…" Bouchaib fingered his beard. His eyes darted first left, then right, and he cleared his throat before he said, "The servant who serves the meals each day has gone to a neighboring town for more men."

"More men?" Omar Ben Ismail asked. "What are you talking about, Bouchaib?"

"They are to work on the Hurani oil rigs. If they, too, should be there, we would be outnumbered."

"That's a big if," Kumar said. "Let's not worry about something that very likely won't happen. Go now and tell the American woman to be prepared. We hit at midnight tomorrow."

"I will tell her, *sidi*."

"What do you think?" Mike asked after Bouchaib had gone. "About the extra men? Will they stay at the Hurani house or go directly to the oil field?"

"I should think they'd go to the oil field." Kumar frowned. "If they do not, we could have a serious problem."

"But one we can handle." Mike got up and began to pace. "What if we planned a little diversion?"

"A diversion?" Abdur looked up from where he was sitting and rubbed a nervous hand across his face. "What do you mean?"

"Let's say that there will be extra men at the Hurani house, oil-rig men. Can the company rigs be seen from the house?"

"Yes," Yassir said. "I saw them when I took Madame Hurani there."

"Okay," Mike went on. "What if there was a fire at one of the rigs? They'd see the fire, wouldn't they? They'd hear the explosion?"

"Yes, Mr. Brennan."

"The minute the Huranis saw it, they'd break their necks getting there, and so would the new rig men."

"Of course!" Kumar shouted. "An oil fire would be devastating. There would be wild confusion..." He got up and began striding up and down the room. "It would be difficult, but not impossible. A couple of our men would start the fire, and when it exploded, we would attack."

"And get Jenny and the boy," Mike said.

He'd be so damn glad when this was over, when he got her out of that dangerous house and safely out of Jahan. That presented another problem, one they hadn't yet discussed.

He turned to Kumar. "What arrangements have been made to get them out of the country?"

"We'll have two Jeeps parked just outside the Hurani compound. As soon as we get in and find Jenny and the boy, we go. It means another trip across the desert toward Zagora, but we'll have all the provisions we need. A few miles before we reach the city, there's a private airstrip. My plane will be waiting there

to take us to my home in Abdu Resaba. You'll have
the exit papers with you; there will be no problem."

"Entry papers?" Mike asked.

"I'm the royal prince of Abdu Resaba, my friend.
I assure you, there will be no difficulty entering my
country. You and your—" he grinned "—your *client*
and her son will stay with me in Abdu Resaba for as
long as you like before you go on to California."

His client. Mike remembered the day Jenny had
walked into his office in Las Vegas, how nervous she'd
been. How determined. He'd told himself when he'd
taken her case that this was strictly business. That he
was doing it for the sixteen grand. But when they'd left
the States, he'd put the money, untouched, into a
Wells Fargo account in both their names. If he needed
it, he'd use it; if he didn't, it would be a new start for
her and the boy.

But first he had to get them safely out of the country.

Mustafa was sure he had seen the girl somewhere
before. But where? Her accent was strange, her manner of speech halting, as though she wasn't sure she
was speaking correctly. Or as though Jahanian wasn't
her first language.

The robe covered her from throat to ankle, the veil
her whole face except her eyes. But he had a feeling
that the robe hid a young, ripe body, the veil a face of
tempting loveliness. That excited him, though he
wasn't sure why.

She wore no head covering. Her hair was black, but
as she had bent to serve him, he could have sworn he'd
seen a single strand of light hair. At the time he had

thought it was the way the sun had struck her face. Now he wondered.

The hands that served had not been the hands of a serving girl. The skin was smooth, the nails well cared for.

The cook said that she was a cousin, a simple girl who had come from Taboku. He wasn't sure he believed that. He'd seen the way she had looked at him when he was attempting to correct his nephew. She had stiffened, and there had been a flash of anger in her wide gray eyes.

Gray eyes. Where had he seen them before?

As night began to fall, Mustafa paced back and forth in the courtyard. Who was she? he asked himself. Where had he seen her before?

He stroked the thick mustache. Tomorrow, he told himself. Tomorrow he would find out who she really was.

Chapter 13

"Abdul won't return until later," Bouchaib told Jenny the next morning. "You'll have to serve again today." He fingered his worry beads and did not look at her or at Seferina when she handed him a glass of hot mint tea.

"What is it?" the older woman asked. "What is troubling you?"

For a moment he didn't answer. His fingers moved nervously over the beads and finally, in a low voice, he said, "Abdul is to bring more men when he comes."

"More men?" Jenny stared at him. "But why?"

"To work in the oil rig." He took a sip of tea and she saw that the hand that held the glass trembled. "This is not good. It's a bad omen. I do not like it."

"They will only pass through here on their way to the oil rig," Seferina said. "Why do you look so frightened, old man?"

"Because tonight Prince Kumar and the American will come. They had expected only a few men to be here defending the house. Now there will be a dozen or more."

A dozen or more. Dear God! "What time do they come?" Jenny asked.

"At midnight." He put down the glass and picked up his worry beads again. "If the men who are to work on the oil rigs arrive after dark, it will be too late to go on. They will have to sleep in the courtyard. How can Prince Kumar and the others slip in through the gate if a dozen men are sleeping here? What will they do? What will happen now? All is lost. It would be madness to go ahead with the plan."

"Do Prince Kumar and Mr. Brennan know of the extra men?" Jenny asked.

"They know."

She struggled to keep her composure. "Then they must have a plan."

"A plan, yes. But it, too, is dangerous."

"What is it, old man?" Seferina prodded.

"They will attempt to start a fire in one of the oil wells. There will be an explosion. It will be a distraction, of course, but that in itself is dangerous." He rubbed a hand across his whiskered chin. "It is their hope that in the confusion, with most of the men running to the fire, they will be able to break into the house to rescue the American woman and the boy." He turned to Jenny. "You must be ready with the boy. Unless things move quickly, the plan will fail. Remember, they will strike just before midnight."

One more day. She had to get through one more day and then it would be over.

As though reading her thoughts, Seferina said, "By tomorrow we will be away from this place. I for one will be glad, for I do not like these people." She looked at Jenny and her face softened. "And you will have your son, *madame.*"

"Yes," Jenny said, "I will have my son." She smiled under the cover of her veil, but the smile faded when she heard the family go into the dining room. She looked at Seferina, then, bracing herself, put glasses of tea on the tray and picked it up.

But before she would leave the kitchen, Seferina placed a cautioning hand on her arm. "Be careful," she whispered. "Remember, it is not over yet. Do not make any mistakes."

Jenny looked into the other woman's troubled eyes. "I won't," she said with more confidence than she felt. And knew that one slip, one word in English, and all would be lost.

Seferina held the door open for her and Jenny went into the dining room.

She placed the tray on the table, went back to the kitchen and returned with a bowl of oranges, thick slices of melon, dates and nuts. That was followed by a *tahine* of chicken cooked with raisins and grapes, and a basket of flat bread.

No one spoke to her. She spoke to no one. Only Timmie smiled up at her. Her heart raced with the knowledge that soon she would be able to tell him who she was.

"This new cook, Seferina, is better than old Ziada," Aiden said. "We must not let her go. When Ziada returns, we will tell her she is no longer needed."

"I agree," Tamar said.

"And what of the serving girl?" Mustafa looked up at Jenny. "Shall we keep her, too? In place of Abdul?"

"Why not?" Aiden smiled up at her. His eyes were kind. "Would you like that, *laeela,* girl?"

"If it would please you, *sidi.*" Jenny lowered her gaze so that he would not see the emotion she suddenly felt, an emotion that came unbidden, unexpected as she remembered the first time she had ever seen Aiden Hurani.

It had been early evening and she had been hurrying across the campus toward the library, her arms loaded with books, when she'd stubbed her toe on a crack in the cement and fallen. The books had scattered; she'd scraped her knee.

"Let me help you," someone called, and she had looked up to see a young man running toward her. "You've hurt yourself," he said. "Your knee is bleeding."

He had helped her up, then he'd picked up her books. "We must do something for your knee," he said as he put an arm around her waist. He took her to the student-union building and when he'd found a chair for her, he'd carefully wiped the blood from her knee and cleaned it with water from the bathroom.

They'd had coffee and talked. He was solicitous and polite, and certainly the most interesting man she'd ever met. She liked his accent almost as much as she liked his dark eyes. He was twenty-three, two years older than she was, and far more worldly than any of the young men she had dated. He had traveled all over the Middle East and Europe, and had studied at the university in Madrid before coming to California. Besides his own language, he spoke French and Spanish as well as English.

Later, when he had walked her back to her dorm, he had asked if she would have dinner with him the following Saturday night. She had said yes, half expecting him to kiss her good-night, but he hadn't.

On Saturday he'd taken her to the town's most expensive restaurant, and later they'd gone dancing. He had been amusing and attentive. To her surprise, he hadn't attempted to kiss her that night, nor on any of the successive nights during the next two weeks. When he finally did, she had all but melted in his arms. When he'd let her go, he said, "We will be married, yes?"

The following weekend she had taken him to Ramona to meet her parents. Her mother had been impressed, her father doubtful.

"Aiden seems like a nice young man," he'd said. "But he comes from a different culture, Jenny. You know nothing about him."

"I know enough," she said with the confidence of her twenty-one years.

"What if he decides to go back to Jahan and take you with him?"

"I'd go, of course," she'd answered. "I love him and he loves me."

What had changed that love? she wondered now. What had turned the charming young man she'd known at school, the man she had fallen in love with, into the abusive man he had become? They had loved each other for a little while; they'd had a child together. What had happened? Where had love gone?

She looked down at him, at the thick black hair with the cowlick exactly like Timmie's, and a feeling of unutterable sadness came over her. In the years she had known him there had been good moments as well as bad, happy memories as well as sad ones. She was going to hurt him, as he had hurt her when he had taken their son away. I'm sorry, she wanted to say. I wish it could have been different. But she said nothing, only served the food and retreated silently to the kitchen.

Everything was in readiness. The two Jeeps had been outfitted with enough gas, food and water to last for the two-day drive across the desert. The men were nervous, restless. Mike paced up and down the room, unable to relax. Only Kumar seemed calm.

"You surprise me," he said to Mike. "You and I have been through far worse battles than what we face tonight. In Saudi Arabia we were in a situation that would have sent lesser men running for the hills. Yet you went into battle as though going for a stroll along the River Seine. And when you were here before, and we got involved in that desert skirmish, I think you actually enjoyed it. Bullets were flying over our heads, scimitars were slashing, and you looked as though you were having the time of your life."

"I was," Mike said. "But this is different."

Kumar nodded. "Because of Jenny."

"Yes, because of her. Because the thought of her being in that house scares the hell out of me."

"One more day, Mike. Then it will be over."

"What if they find out who she is before we go in?"

"Jenny's a smart girl. If she stays in the kitchen and keeps her head down, she'll be all right."

"And if she doesn't?" Mike's face twisted with the agony of fear. He turned in his pacing. "It's all set?"

he asked. "The men have everything they need to start the fire?"

Kumar nodded. "Yassir and Omar know what they're supposed to do."

"The rigs will be guarded."

"They know that. They'll handle it."

"They go in at eleven-thirty."

"Yes, Mike. That gives them half an hour to take care of the guards and start the fire. It will catch quickly and there'll be an explosion."

"Will they be able to get away in time? I don't want them hurt."

"They're good men, they know what to do." Kumar reached for a cigarette. "The minute we see the explosion, we hit the house. There'll be three of us against the three of them." Kumar grinned. "As you say in English, it will be a cinch."

A cinch. Mike wished he believed that.

He went out to check the two Jeeps. The tins of gasoline weren't strapped to the sides as they'd been when they made the trip here, but were secured on the floor of the back seat, hopefully protected in case of gunfire. There were gallon jugs of water, canteens, tins of food, some fruit. Enough to last them until they got to the private landing strip. There was a bedroll for Jenny and the boy. No tent, because there wasn't room in the Jeep.

At four that afternoon they gathered to go over the plans one final time.

"Yassir and Omar will take one of the Jeeps and leave here at eleven-fifteen," Mike said. "That'll give them time to get to the wells. As soon as they start the fire, they head back to the Huranis'. By that time the oil-rig men will have taken off and we'll be inside the house. As soon as we get Jenny and the boy, Kumar and I leave with them. The rest of you take the second Jeep and follow us."

"The Huranis will go to the police," Abdur pointed out. "They'll be after us."

"That'll take time," Mike said. "And remember, it'll be dark. That's to our advantage."

"It's also a disadvantage." Kumar's expression was thoughtful. "It's dangerous to drive in the desert at night. Even with headlights it will be difficult to see the road. If there's a storm and wind sweeps across the dunes, the road will be invisible. That's a danger and it worries me."

"You're talking about a sandstorm?" Mike asked.

"Alize," Kumar said. "Yes. If it comes it will wipe out the road."

"And make us harder to find." Mike shook his head. "You know yourself that the chances of such a storm are slim. We have enough to worry about, so let's just forget it."

"And pray to Allah that it does not happen," Kumar murmured.

Mustafa could not get the thought of the serving girl out of his mind. There was something about her that reminded him of someone. But who? He liked the graceful way she walked, the way she used her hands. No simple village girl would move as she moved. No simple village girl had eyes like the pale underbelly of a dove.

He was a man of strong sexual appetites, a man who took his pleasure when he was here in Al Hamaan with the more expensive of the dancing girls who worked in the bars inside the souk. When he was in Paris or

Rome he sought out only the high-class call girls he arranged for through an agency. He had no interest in a real relationship, no desire for a wife. All that he had ever wanted was a woman to satisfy the urgent cravings of his body. The women he chose must be clean, young, well formed and, of course, beautiful. He took them, he paid them, and once he was through with them he did not see them again.

Only once had the idea of marriage crossed his mind, but the woman had been forbidden to him because she had been his brother's wife. His desire for her had been like a fever in the blood. There had been times when he'd wanted to take her even though he knew it was *haram*. Several years had passed since last he had seen her, but there were times when he still thought of her, of how it would be to force her to submit to him, to make her his for as long as he wanted her. Each time the thought of her came to him there had been a feeling of regret at having missed what he instinctively knew would have been a memorable experience.

Aiden had been no match for her, but he himself would have been. He would have taken her, tamed her, pleasured himself to exhaustion, and made her his wife so she could never escape.

He had not felt that kind of sexual excitement in a long time, but he had felt it the first time he had looked at the serving girl. If she was the cousin of Seferina, just a girl from a remote village, then he could, of course, take her by force. If she was not, he would figure out a way to have her.

But first he must find out who she really was. Then he would decide how to go about satisfying himself with her.

He smiled and a plan began to form.

He called one of the servants. "Bring the woman Seferina to me," he ordered. And when she came he said, "I would like you to prepare a special dish to-night—*sambusak*. I would also like baby lamb cooked with sesame seeds and mushrooms from Zagora."

A look of concern crossed Seferina's face. "We have no lamb, *sidi*. And the mushrooms will be hard to find."

"But you will find them, yes?" He scowled. "Take the new girl and go to the market. Ask until you find what I want." He waved her away. "Go at once. Do you hear?"

"Yes, *sidi*," she said. And bowed her way out.

He watched from the window, and when the two women were out of sight, he went to the small bedroom off the kitchen where they slept. There was a narrow bed where the cook slept, and a straight-backed chair with a blanket neatly folded over the back of it. On the seat was a black scarf that had been knotted to hold extra clothes. One of Seferina's robes hung from a nail on the wall. On another nail there was a smaller robe.

He looked around, frowning, not sure what it was he was looking for. His gaze rested on the chair and the blanket there. Undoubtedly the new girl slept on the blanket on the floor. Then the scarf was hers.

He picked it up, untied it, reached in and drew out a pair of silk-and-lace panties. Silk and lace for a village girl? He laughed. Not likely. What else did this mysterious woman have in her bag? A lacy brassiere. He picked up the bra and ran his thick fingers over the lace. His nostrils thinned and he had to bite his lip to hold back the quick flare of passion that hardened his body—passion that made him forget for a moment that no ordinary village girl would have such finery. He looked at the label on the inside of the bra. What in the name of Allah...? He sucked in his breath. The label read California Girl.

With a muttered oath he dumped the contents of the scarf out on the chair. A brush, a comb, a toy giraffe. A giraffe? Why in the name of all that was holy would she carry a child's toy? He stared at it, puzzled. Then, like a stab to his gut, he knew. It had belonged to Aiden's boy.

"*Zfft!*" Mustafa flung the toy animal across the room. It was *her*, by Allah! Jenny! His brother's wife! The woman who haunted his dreams. She had come to steal her son!

He said a fervent prayer to damn her to eternal hell, and vowed that he himself would send her on her way. But first...

He put his hand over his groin and felt the terrible hardness there. But first he would do all of the things he had ever dreamed of doing to her.

He put the bra and panties, the brush and comb back into the black scarf and tied it. But he kept the orange giraffe.

And smiled, knowing how terrified she would be when she discovered it was missing.

The wind started a little after ten that night.

Abdur was the first to notice. He was on his way to load the explosives into the Jeep when he stopped. "Wait," he said to Omar Ben Ismail. "Listen."

The other man looked at him curiously. "What is it?"

"*Alize*," Abdur said. "The wind of the desert."

"I hear nothing."

"Turn your face to the west. You will feel it."

Omar turned his face as he had been bidden. "Perhaps..." He wet his lips and his eyes in the darkness were squeezed tight with concern. "Perhaps it is only a breeze from the desert."

"This is no breeze. A wind is coming. We must tell the others."

Mike, Kumar and Yassir were seated on the floor when the two men returned to the house. Youssef Madih had just given Mike the forged exit papers that would get him, Jenny and the boy out of the country.

"A windstorm is coming," Abdur told Kumar.

Kumar looked up. "What? What did you say?"

"*Alize, sidi*. It comes from the west."

"Are you sure?"

"As sure as I am standing here telling you about it."

"What's he saying?" Mike asked, not quite positive that he'd understood, hoping he hadn't.

"A windstorm." Kumar stood. "This is bad, Mike."

"How long will it last if it comes?"

"A day, a week." Kumar shook his head. "With an *alize* it is hard to say. I think..." His eyebrows came together in a frown. "I think we must postpone the attack until tomorrow or the day after. Until the storm passes."

"No!" Mike got up and faced his friend. "I want Jenny out of there tonight."

"I know how you feel, Mike, but be reasonable. If the storm turns out to be a bad one, we'll barely be able to see what we're doing. As for driving..." He shook his head. "We won't even be able to see the road. It's too dangerous. We must delay."

"No, dammit, I won't delay. If you won't go with me, I'll go in alone."

"I won't let you do that."

Mike turned toward him. His face was hard with determination, as though set in stone. "Try and stop me," he said.

The two men glared at each other. Then Mike said, "Look, Kumar, maybe we can use the storm to our advantage. Sure, it's going to be difficult to see where we're going, but it'll be difficult for them, too. They won't be able to follow us."

"You've never seen a desert storm," Kumar said. "It's like being in a tropical typhoon, only instead of rain, it is the sand that blinds you, that clogs your nostrils and makes breathing almost impossible. The wind tears at your clothes, and even if you're strong, you must bend over double to walk. What roads there are become impassable. Dunes shift, animals and people are buried. All anyone can do is seek shelter and wait until it's over."

"I won't wait," Mike said fiercely. "I can't."

"Another thing we must think about," Kumar went on. "If the storm hits tonight, the men hired to work on the oil rigs won't be able to leave. They'll have to stay at the Huranis'. That could mean we'd be fighting maybe a dozen men." His voice grew stern. "We can't do it, Mike. We'd be taking too big of a chance."

There was a part of Mike that knew he was being unreasonable. Kumar was a desert man. If he said a storm was coming, then it was coming. And he was right about the odds. A dozen or more against the four of them? He'd been up against odds like that before and it didn't scare him. But the thought of Jenny and her boy being in the middle of it did. Kumar was right;

the sensible thing would be to wait a day or two until the storm had passed.

But he couldn't wait. He didn't know why, he only knew that he couldn't let Jenny stay where she was for another night, another day. He had to get her out of there.

"I know you're right," he said to Kumar. "Everything you say makes sense. But I can't wait. If you don't want to go with me, then I'll do it alone. I know, somehow, Kumar, I *know* I have to get her out of there tonight."

"I will go with you, Mr. Brennan," Yassir said.

"Thank you, Yassir."

"Madness," Youssef Madih mumbled. "It is madness to go out in an *alize*."

"Then I, too, am mad." Kumar held his hand out to Mike. "You are a fool, my friend. But because you *are* my friend I will not let you go alone." He looked at the other men. "I won't order you to accompany us. The decision is yours."

Omar Ben Ismail and Abdur looked at each other. "We go," they said in unison.

"And do we still blow up an oil rig?" Yassir asked.

Mike hesitated. "Yes," he said at last. "Even with the storm, we'll need whatever distraction we can get." He reached out and shook each man's hand. "Tonight," he said.

And it was settled.

By eleven-thirty the wind had risen to a screaming pitch. All the windows and shutters in the house had been closed and locked. But still the sand drifted in.

"They won't come tonight," Seferina said.

She and Jenny were in the small bedroom they shared. For the last hour Jenny had been pacing, hoping and praying the wind would stop. But it hadn't stopped; it had grown worse.

Abdul had returned two hours ago. The men he had brought with him had crowded into the sitting room. They would not leave until the storm passed.

"It would be madness to strike tonight." Seferina sat on the edge of her bed. "You must ease yourself, *madame.* I assure you they will not come."

"If Mike said he would, then he will."

"How can you be sure? No man with sense in his head would be out tonight. Let us rest now. Tomorrow, if the storm has passed, Bouchaib will come and tell us what we are to do."

"I can't rest." Jenny looked at her watch. It was fifteen minutes before twelve. "I've got to go," she said. "I'll wait outside Timmie's room until I hear gunfire. If there is no gunfire, if the men don't come tonight, I'll return."

"If they catch you it will ruin everything," Seferina wailed. "They will kill us all. You must listen to me, *madame.* You must—"

But Jenny wouldn't listen. Mike had said they would strike at midnight. She was sure that he would, and she had to be ready.

"Don't go to bed," she told Seferina. "Be ready to leave as soon as you hear anything."

She picked up the black head scarf that she'd put on the chair. She had the photographs hidden in the pocket of her robe, and she would show them to Timmie so he wouldn't be frightened. But just in case, she'd give him the giraffe, too. He'd recognize it. He would remember and know that he was safe.

It was almost time. She had to hurry. She untied the bundle, but when she reached in for the giraffe, her expression went blank. The breath stopped in her throat.

With a murmured cry, she dumped the contents of the scarf out on the chair.

"My God," she whispered. "My God!"

The giraffe wasn't there. Someone had taken it.

Chapter 14

Jenny stared at the things scattered on the chair. Tentacles of fear clawed at her insides; the shock was so great she felt for a moment as though she were going to faint.

Somebody had taken the giraffe. Somebody knew.

"What is it?" Seferina asked, sounding frightened.

Jenny straightened. If she told Seferina what had happened—that someone had been in this room, someone knew who she was and very likely why she was here—Seferina would panic. She couldn't let that happen. The other woman was frightened as it was. This would send her over the edge.

She didn't need that now. She had to have her wits about her. So she made herself say, "Nothing's wrong. I—I guess I'm just a little tense because it's time to go." She retied the scarf. "Remember, as soon as you hear gunshots, or the explosion, go into the court-yard."

"But the wind!" Seferina wailed. "I'm afraid of the *alize.*"

"You can't stay here." Jenny hurried to the bed and put a hand on the older woman's shoulder. "I have to go now," she said. "Don't be frightened. It's going to be all right. I'll wait until a little after midnight. If the men don't come, I'll return."

But they had to come, because someone knew, someone was waiting, playing a terrible cat-and-mouse game. Tomorrow might be too late; she had to escape tonight.

Kumar had been right—they could barely see the road that led out of town toward the Huranis'. The other Jeep, with Abdur and Yassir, had left thirty minutes ago. The men would be at the rigs by now. Would they be able to do what they had to do in this wind? Would they be able to start a fire? And if they did, would they be able to escape before everything blew?

He thought of Abdur. The man was too heavy. Would he be able to run, to get away in time? And young Yassir with his dark soulful eyes that told all that he was feeling. Yassir, whom he could not blame for falling under Jenny's spell. Would he survive? Would any of them?

The sand swept across the desert, howling like an evil spirit descended from hell. It splashed across the glare of the headlights, an almost solid wall, choking the men inside the Jeep, making visibility all but impossible.

Kumar had been right; it was madness to attack in the middle of a sandstorm. But they had to, for Jenny's sake. So far she had been able to pull this off, but how long could she continue? Another day? Another night before one of the Huranis discovered her true identity? No, it had to be tonight. He had to get to her before it was too late.

Mike peered through the swirl of sand, his hands clenched, his gut knotted with fear. Not for himself, not for the battle that lay ahead, but for Jenny. Because he loved her and because he knew, somewhere deep inside him, that every moment she spent in the Hurani house she was in danger. Terrible danger.

The windshield wipers were useless. Kumar, at the wheel, uttered ancient Jahanian curses as he peered through the darkness and tried to stay on the road. "We can't go in until we see the fire," he shouted to Mike above the roar of the wind. "We'll have to park and wait until we see it."

He knew Kumar was right, that if they went in before the explosion, there would be too many against them. They had to wait, but, my God, this was the worst torture he had ever known.

Kumar stopped the Jeep. "We can't stay here for too long," he said. "If we do we'll be swamped in sand, we'll never get out."

So they waited, engine idling, nerves raw, eyes searching the darkness for a sign of light, the roar of a fire above the roar of the wind. Mike wanted to plunge ahead, wanted to go single-handedly into the Hurani house, gun blazing, fighting his way to Jenny. But he couldn't; he had to sit here and wait.

"There!" Omar Ben Ismail cried. "To the left. I see the fire! They've done it! They've fired the rig!"

It shot straight up, bright orange through the hail of sand. There was a shout from the house and men came out and headed for the fire. Mike slapped Kumar on the back. "Go!" he shouted over the roar of the wind. "Go!"

Jenny slipped through the dining room. At the entrance to the hall that led to the bedrooms, she waited, listening. The only sound was the terrible, screaming wind. It frightened her, for she knew how dangerous it was, how difficult it would be to travel in a storm like this.

Perhaps Seferina had been right, perhaps Mike and Kumar had postponed the attack. She hesitated. If there had been a delay, wouldn't Mike have found a way to notify her? But what if that had been impossible?

Should she go forward or should she return to the room she shared with Seferina and wait? No, Mike had said he would come tonight. She had to go on, and hope and pray that he would come. Because she knew she could not stay another moment in this house.

Who had suspected her? Who had searched her room? Aiden? His father? Mustafa? At the thought that it might be Mustafa who lay in wait for her, she felt the sickness of fear rise in her throat.

But fear or not, she would go on, she would not be deterred from getting her son. If it was Mustafa who had taken the toy, then he was waiting for her to discover the loss. He would be in no hurry to confront her. He'd want her to worry about it, think about it until she was sick with fear. But when he did confront her...

Jenny's mouth went dry and she started to shake. There could be no delay; it had to be tonight. She had to find Timmie and get him away from here before Mustafa or whoever it was who had been in her room discovered she was gone.

The sound of her footfalls in the hall were muffled by the cry of the wind. At the door of Aiden's room she paused, and as she had yesterday, felt a twist of emotion. He loved their son as much as she did. He had been wrong to take Timmie away from her and that was hard to forgive. But because of her own anguish when she had lost her son, she knew how Aiden would feel when he discovered she had taken him. That saddened her, but it did not weaken her resolve.

She stopped in front of Timmie's room. In a moment she would be with him. Would he be frightened by her sudden appearance? How could she assure him? How could she quickly make him believe that she was his mother, that she had come for him at last? She thought for a moment, then pulled the wig off and ran her fingers through the short blond curls.

I'm your mama, she would tell him. I've come to take you home. She'd close the door and light the lamp and show him the photographs, then she'd gather him up in her robe to protect him from the storm and carry him out to the courtyard, where Seferina waited.

She took a step forward. Only a moment more and she would have him in her arms again. Only a moment . . .

A different sound, not the wind, made her hesitate. She turned. The dark shadow loomed only a few feet away. Before she could cry out or move, he had her, one hand clamped over her mouth, the other around her waist.

He dragged her backward. Terrified, she tried to bite his fingers, but he gripped her so hard she couldn't. She struggled, bringing her elbows back, striking his chest, kicking to reach his legs. But he wouldn't let her go. He drew her backward, into his room, and kicked the door shut.

She couldn't see in the darkness, but she knew who it was, knew that it was Mustafa even before he reached for the bedside light and snapped it on.

"So it is you!" He laughed, and the sound of it was even more horrifying than the wind that howled outside. He gripped her wrists with one hand and with the other hand reached to touch her hair. "Like gold," he whispered. "Just as I remembered."

"Let me go!" Jenny tried to break free of the hand that held her wrists, but he tightened his hold, twisted, hurting her, and she cried out in pain.

"What are you doing here?" He shook her. "Tell me!" he cried. "How did you get here? Who is helping you?"

"No one," she managed to say. "I came here alone."

"Liar! How did you come to work in the kitchen? It was the new cook who helped you, wasn't it? The woman Seferina? But not her alone. There has to be someone else. Someone who got you into the country. Someone who planned this." His face was only inches from hers. "Tell me," he whispered. "Tell me or by Allah I will—"

"It was me. Only me." She tried to twist away from him. "I had help before I came to Jahan, but once I was here I was on my own."

"Don't lie to me!" He struck her across the face. Her head snapped back and she would have fallen had he not been holding her.

He fastened a hand in her hair and brought her face close to his. "I'll find out. By the time I'm through with you, you'll be only too happy to tell me everything I want to know."

She felt his breath on her face, the hardness of his body so close to hers.

"But first," he said, "you and I have some unfinished business." He dragged her toward his bed. "Do you know how long I've waited to take you? How many nights I've dreamed about you? About what it would be like when at last I had you?" He shoved her down and pinned her with his arms. His face was only inches from hers. "Every time I took a woman I pretended she was you," he went on. "There have been times when I've screamed your name in that final moment, and I've beaten the woman because she wasn't you."

Fear paralyzed Jenny and sickness rose in her throat. She couldn't let this happen. She had to fight, fight . . .

He fastened one hand at the top of her robe and ripped it open to her stomach. His eyes narrowed with desire. "You're everything I knew you would be. Your breasts are like ripe pomegranates, soft and sweetly round, waiting for my lips to suckle. Waiting—"

She struck out and caught him a glancing blow on the side of his head. Before he could grab her again, she raised her knee. But he was too quick for her. He twisted fast and her knee caught his thigh.

"She cat!" He grabbed her wrists again. "How I will enjoy taming you. But first..." He raised his robe and she saw that he wore nothing beneath it.

She screamed. Screamed until the sound of it carried over the screeching howl of the wind. Until she thought her lungs would burst, the lining of her throat would tear.

She felt his hot breath against her mouth, the moist lips, his tongue. She fought as she had never fought before, heaving her body up under his, frantic in the need to get away. He tightened a hand on her breast, hurting her. He said words in Jahanian she didn't understand. His big body began to move against hers and he reached to lift her robe.

She freed one hand and raked her nails across his face. He cursed and struck her so hard on the side of her head that for a moment everything went black. As though in the distance she heard a roar, a burst of sound that shook the house. And knew she was losing consciousness.

The door to Mustafa's room opened. "There's an explosion at one of the oil rigs," Aiden cried. "We've got to get out there. We..." He stopped. "My God!" he said. "What are you doing? How dare you bring a woman here to our father's house? Is it the serving girl? Let her go at once."

"Aiden!" With the last bit of her strength, Jenny cried his name. "Aiden, help me!"

His head jerked up. "What...? Who...?" He ran to the bed. "Jenny? Oh, my God, Jenny!" He looked from her to his brother, then his eyes went wild and he leapt at Mustafa, grabbed him by his throat and pulled him away from Jenny. "I'll kill you," he panted. "Kill you!"

Mustafa flung him away. "Get out of here," he screamed. "You were no match for her, not man enough to hold her. But I am, and by all that's holy, I will have her."

Another explosion rent the air. Mustafa whirled. "What is it?" he cried. "What's happening?"

"We're blowing you to hell and back!" Mike, his gun leveled straight at Mustafa's belly, stood in the doorway. His gaze swept the three of them: Aiden, Mustafa, Jenny. Her robe was ripped halfway down the front. There was a bruise on her face. Her eyes were dazed, wide with terror.

He looked at Mustafa. "Oh, you son of a bitch," he said in a voice soft with menace. "You sorry son of a bitch."

Quick as a cat, Mustafa reached into his robe. The blade of a knife glittered in the light when he drew his arm back to throw. Mike fired. Mustafa staggered back, turned as though to run, then fell facedown.

Mike aimed the gun at Aiden. "You're next!" he said.

"No!" Jenny struggled to sit up. "Don't," she pleaded. "Mike, don't. He didn't know. He tried to stop Mustafa."

The gun finger twitched. He wanted to kill, was ready to kill. This was the man who had beaten and abused her. The man who had stolen her child. His finger tightened on the trigger.

"Mike, please." She was crying now. "Please."

He hesitated, and when he did, Aiden flung himself at him. They struggled. Aiden made a grab for the gun; Mike pulled back and clubbed him across the side of his head. Aiden fell without a sound.

Mike ran to Jenny. He pulled her to him, rough in his need to know that she was all right. "Did he hurt you?" he cried. "Are you all right? Did he . . . ?"

Shudder after shudder ran through her body. Her legs felt weak and she was dizzy from the blow she'd taken. "No," she was able to say. "Aiden stopped him." She looked down at the man who had been her husband. "Is he all right? Is he—"

"I didn't kill him, if that's what you mean."

"Mustafa? Is he dead?"

"I hope so." He helped her stand. "We've got to get out of here," he said urgently. "Where's the boy's room?"

"Across the hall."

"Are you all right? Can you make it?"

"Yes." She clutched Mike's hand. "Maybe Timmie heard the noise. If he did he'll be frightened."

"Take it easy, we'll get him."

He put his arm around her and led her out of the room into the hall. She opened the door of her son's room. Mike took a flashlight out of his pocket and turned it on.

"Who's there?" a frightened voice asked. "Is that you, *Pedar,* Father?"

"No, baby," Jenny said in English. "It's Mama, Timmie."

"Mama?"

She ran across the room, so eager to touch him she couldn't hold back. "Darling," she said, "Oh, Timmie."

He shrank against the head of his bed and began to cry. "I want my father," he wept in Jahanian. "Where's my father?"

"Timmie..." She turned an anguished face to Mike. "He doesn't know me," she said. "He doesn't remember."

"Hold on." Mike found the overhead light and turned it on.

Timmie covered his eyes with his hands. "Go away!" he cried. "I want my father."

"Oh, Timmie..." Jenny took the photographs out of the pocket of her robe. "Look," she said, and gently took his hands from his eyes. "Look, darling. This is Mama and Timmie. Remember, sweetheart? This was your room. There's Jerry Giraffe sitting in his chair. And here's a picture of Grandma and Grandpa. And your pony. Remember the pony Grandpa bought for you? You named him Giddap. Remember?"

He didn't answer, but now the hands were lowered and he was looking at the pictures. Jenny kept talking, showing him the pictures over and over again, saying, "It's Timmie and Mama. Remember? Timmie and Mama."

"We've got to get out of here," Mike said.

"I don't want to take him by force." She touched the top of her son's head. "I've missed you so much," she said.

He looked up at her. "Mama?"

"Yes, baby." She hadn't cried before, not when she was afraid, not when Mustafa had hurt her. But she was crying now. She put her arms around him. "Mama's come to take you home," she said. "Back to Grandma and Grandpa. Would you like that?"

"Uh-huh." He tightened his arms around her neck. "I was always missing you," he said. "Sometimes I cried because I was missing you."

"Me, too, baby." Jenny hugged him close. "Me, too."

"Is Father coming with us?"

"No, Timmie. But he can come and visit us sometime." She held him away from her. "This is Mr. Brennan. He's going to make sure we get home."

"Hi, kid," Mike said. "Where're your clothes?"

Timmie looked at him uncertainly. "On the chair," he whispered.

"Get him dressed." Mike went to the door. "I don't like it. I've got a feeling all hell is going to break loose any minute. Hurry it up."

Jenny grabbed the white robe up off the chair and put it over Timmie's head. Then she put his sandals on and picked him up. "There's a storm," she said as she wrapped her arms around him. "A lot of wind and sand, Timmie, so when we get outside I'm going to cover your face. But don't be scared. I'm right here and so is Mr. Brennan."

The boy shot Mike a doubtful look and his lower lip trembled.

"Let's go!" Mike snapped. He started out of the door. "Stay behind me," he told Jenny. "If I tell you to drop, drop. If I tell you to run, run. Got it?"

He didn't wait for an answer. He started down the hall. Now that the explosions had stopped, the only sound was the roar of the wind. He didn't like it. He had a feeling in his gut that something was wrong. The hairs on the back of his neck were standing at attention. Something...

Suddenly, out of the dark, a figure lunged at him, and in the light of his flashlight he saw the flash of a knife.

He grabbed the arm of the man with the knife, twisted hard and heard bone snap. The man cried out and clutched his wrist. As he went down, a second man leapt out of the darkness, smashing into Mike with the force of a bulldozer. The flashlight spun out of Mike's hand. He fought for a foothold, tried to thrust the body away from his, drew back a fist and smashed it into his attacker's face. The man reeled, struck out and smacked Mike's ear. Mike hit the wall, slumped, shook his head, then, bending low, rushed at the man and barreled into him. They hit the floor. Mike swung, caught his opponent on the chin, hit him twice, a third time, and the man lay still.

Mike crawled to his feet just in time to hear Jenny scream a warning. He snapped his head around and saw, in the light from the room at the end of the hall, an old man, his face a mask of rage, rushing toward him, a long-barreled gun in his hand.

Mike threw back his arm to sweep Jenny and the boy aside. He felt the hot force of the bullet crease his shoulder and spun to the side as though he'd been hit by a ten-ton truck. Before the old man could fire again, Mike brought his arm up and delivered a karate chop to the side of his neck.

"Come on!" He grabbed Jenny's sleeve and pulled her after him. "Let's get the hell out of here."

They raced down the hall, through the dining room. Where had the extra men come from? Were there other workers who hadn't left when the fire started? What in the hell was going on?

Above the cry of the wind he heard gunshots. "Where are we?" he called back over his shoulder to Jenny. "How do we get out of here?"

"Through the courtyard." She pushed past him, leading the way now, into the kitchen, through the door to the outside.

The wind hit them and they staggered back. Mike grasped her arms. Timmie was crying. She covered his face in the folds of her robe.

"The Jeep," he yelled close to her ear. "We've got to get to the Jeep." He had his gun out, holding it in front of him like a shield. He saw shadowy figures, indistinguishable in the swirl of the wind. "Kumar!" he yelled. "Kumar!"

"Here!" One of the figures loomed out of the darkness. "More men than we thought," Kumar shouted. "We'll hold them off. Get Jenny and the boy to the Jeep."

"I'll be back." With his arms around Jenny and the boy, Mike started toward the Jeep.

"No," Kumar cried. "Go on." A shot whizzed over his head. "Go!" he yelled. "We'll be right behind you."

"I can't leave you," Mike shouted. He let go of Jenny to turn back to Kumar, but when he did, a blast of wind hit her and knocked her and the boy down. He pulled them back up. He couldn't leave her; he couldn't leave his friend. What was he going to do?

He could hear the boy's frantic cries over the screaming wind, and knew Jenny and the kid couldn't manage alone.

Just then Omar Ben Ismail appeared next to Kumar. "We've got them," he said. "*Balak!* Let's move out!"

"Seferina?" Jenny cried. "Where is Seferina?"

"She got away, she's safe," Omar said.

They backed away, Mike holding Jenny and the boy behind them. "You and Jenny take the first Jeep," Kumar shouted. "We'll be right behind you in the second one." He clapped Mike on the shoulder. "Go," he ordered. "We'll follow."

They bent double trying to get to the Jeep. He got her and the boy in, ran around and jumped in on his side. The key was in the ignition. He turned it, gunned the motor, and the vehicle leapt forward.

"Stay down," he told her when he heard shots behind him. "Keep the kid covered."

He zoomed onto what he thought was the road. Even with the headlights on high beam he couldn't see, but he kept going. Once he looked back, hoping to see the lights of the other Jeep, but there was only darkness and swirling sand. He told himself he'd see the lights of the town soon, then he'd know where he was.

He couldn't make out the road, only hoped and prayed he was still on it. It was hard going. Piles of sand had drifted, blocking the way. A bigger drift stopped him. He cursed, shot into reverse and managed to get around it.

They should have been in Al Hamaan by now. Dammit, where was the town? Once again he looked over his shoulder, searching through the maelstrom of sand for a light. Nothing. Nothing but darkness and blowing sand.

He tried to see Jenny. Got enough of a glimpse to see that she'd tied a scarf over her nose and her mouth. He took one hand off the wheel and tightened it around her knee. "It'll be all right," he hollered over the sound of the wind.

Her hand covered his and squeezed hard. "Al Hamaan?" she asked. "Where is it?"

"Soon," he said. "We should see it soon."

But he knew they wouldn't. They were lost. All they could do was keep going and hope they would find a village. Or that Kumar's Jeep would find them.

Chapter 15

An hour went by. Mike kept driving, searching for the lights of a town, a car, something. But there was only darkness, the wind and the terrible, swirling sand.

Jenny had slumped down in the seat. He didn't know if she was asleep or merely so battered by the storm she could no longer keep her head up. Kumar had said it was madness to come out in the storm, and he'd been right. But if they hadn't come tonight, if they hadn't attacked when they had...

He tightened his hands on the wheel. He would never forget the sight of Jenny on the bed, her robe torn, her eyes wide with fear; the man Mustafa, his face distorted with passion and anger. Mike hoped he'd killed the son of a bitch.

And Aiden. He wondered if Jenny was still in love with her ex-husband. She'd been married to him for six years. Maybe, in spite of the fact that he'd abused her, she still cared about him. Maybe that's why she'd stopped him from shooting Aiden.

He found his thoughts drifting like the sand and bit down hard on his bottom lip to bring himself back into focus. He was going less than twenty miles an hour now, unsure of where he was headed. The wind gritted in his teeth, stuck in his nose. He squinted his eyes, trying to see Jenny. He knew she must be suffering.

What could he do? What in the hell could he do? If he stopped, they'd never be able to start again. He had to keep going, but where? Where in the hell were they?

The Jeep sloughed to the left, caught in a high drift of sand. He shoved the gear stick into reverse and tried to back up. The wheels spun, and they only sank deeper in the sand. He shot the vehicle into first gear and turned the wheel sharply to try to go around the high drift. The Jeep didn't move; they were stuck.

"What is it?" Jenny asked. "Why are we stopping?"

"We're stuck." Mike opened his door. "I'm going to try to dig us out."

The wind hit him so hard he had to hang on to the side of the vehicle to keep from blowing away. He struggled to the front of the Jeep. In the dim glow of the headlights he saw that the sand was three feet deep around the front tires. There was no way in hell he could get out of here, but he had to try.

He knelt down and started scooping the sand away with his hands. It wasn't any use; the more he scooped the more the sand drifted back. He struggled to the back of the Jeep. It was worse there. They were mired in. There was no way out.

He climbed back into the Jeep. Jenny's face, except for her eyes, was covered. She looked terrified.

"Can't we get out?" she cried above the noise of the wind.

"There's no way," he said.

"What are we going to do?"

"Wait till this passes. When daylight comes, when the wind stops, we'll dig it out."

She looked down at Timmie. He'd been asleep, but he was awake now.

"I want to go home," he said in Jahanian. "I don't like it here." He started to cry.

"Shh," she said. "Shh, Timmie. It's going to be all right. We're just going to stay here for a little while, and as soon as the storm is over, we'll leave."

"No!" he wailed. "I don't want to stay here. I want my father. I want—"

"Can it, kid!" Mike snapped. "And speak English."

Timmie looked at him, so startled he stopped crying. His chin trembled. He moved closer to Jenny.

"Really," she said, "he's only a little boy. You can't expect—"

"I expect him to behave himself and stop whining. I know this isn't much fun, but you're not a baby, kid, so don't act like one. When morning comes we'll get out of here. We'll find a road and pretty soon we'll get to an airport and fly you and your mom back home."

"We're going on an airplane?"

"Yeah."

"When?"

"As soon as we get the he…as soon as we're out of here."

Timmie thrust his chin out. "I wanna go now!" he yelled.

Mike glared at the boy. "Then go!"

Timmie shot him a look, then buried his face against Jenny's breast. "I don't like him," he whispered.

Neither did she at that moment. Holding her little boy close, she tried to slide as far over on the seat as she could. But Mike wouldn't let her. He put his arms around her and Tim and held them close.

"We'll ride this out together," he said close to her ear. "Try to get some sleep. I have a hunch it's going to be even rougher tomorrow."

She wanted to move away, but he held her there, she and her son, clasped in his arms. A unit of three, huddled close against the storm that raged all about them.

Kumar and his men reached Al Hamaan. Omar had taken a bullet in his arm; Yassir's face had been scorched in the fire and his arms had been burned. But they'd made it. As soon as the storm abated, they'd head toward Zagora and safety. He'd ride with Mike and Jenny and her boy, his men would follow.

But where in the hell was Mike? All the way from the Hurani house he'd been searching the darkness for the taillights of the other Jeep. Driving had been bad, dangerous. As soon as they were out of shooting distance, he'd slowed to a crawl. Abdur had taken the flashlight and walked in front of the vehicle so they wouldn't stray from the road.

He'd prayed to Allah that when they reached Youssef Madih's he'd find Mike and Jenny already there. But they hadn't been. Where were they? If Mike had gotten off the road—if, instead of heading for Al Hamaan, he'd gone into the desert—then he was lost.

The thought shook Kumar. He knew the desert because he was a desert man. Mike wasn't. He was brave and he was courageous, but he was no match for an *alize* like this. When the storm abated, the face of the desert would have changed. There would be no road, no landmark, only mile after mile of sand.

Kumar's face grew pale. Mike and Jenny and her son were out there somewhere in the terrible swirl of wind and sand. He said a silent prayer that Allah would protect them.

Mike awakened to silence. In the first faint light of dawn he opened his eyes to the vast stretches of desert land. There was nothing else, only sand, rising dunes and a gray sky that would soon lighten to the heat of the day.

Jenny was asleep, the boy still clasped in her arms. When he stirred, the kid opened his eyes. He looked at Mike, not recognizing him.

"Hi," Mike said. "Are you hungry?"

Timmie nodded without speaking.

"Okay, we can take care of that." He touched Jenny's shoulder. "Jen?" he said. "Jen, it's time to wake up."

She murmured sleepily and opened her eyes. Tim patted her face. "I'm hungry, Mama," he said.

She hugged him, then looked at Mike and said, "We have food, don't we?"

"Sure." He tried to open the Jeep, but the sand came halfway up the door, so he eased himself out over it. And knew when he did that there was no way they were doing to drive out of here. The Jeep was mired deep in sand, and even if it hadn't been, there was no road, nothing for as far as he could see. It was a miracle he'd been able to drive for as long as he had.

Trying not to reveal the knot of fear in his belly, he reached into the back seat. The tarp they'd put over the tins of gas, the food and water, was covered with sand piled a foot high. He got the cover off, shook the sand away and took out a canteen of water.

"Here you are," he said when he'd taken the stopper out. He handed it to the boy.

Tim took the canteen, and when he tilted it up to drink, Jenny looked at Mike over the boy's head. "How bad is it?" she asked.

"Bad enough."

"Can we get the Jeep out?"

He shook his head. "We're going to have to hoof it."

"Walk?" she said. "You want us to walk?" She looked at the sea of sand that surrounded them. "We can't. We'll never make it."

"We can't stay here. We've got food and water, the tarp for shelter when we rest, and a compass. Once Kumar discovers we didn't reach Al Hamaan, he'll be out looking for us."

And so would the Huranis. Aiden and his father and their men would start a search. And Mustafa? Damn! Mike mentally kicked himself for not making sure that Aiden's brother was dead. Mustafa was the strong one. If he was alive, he wouldn't rest until he found them.

Jenny took a drink from the canteen. When she passed it to Mike, she saw the dried blood on his shirt.

"You're hurt!" she said, alarmed.

"It's only a crease." He took a sip of water. The sun would be up soon; the temperature would climb. They'd need the water then.

He climbed into the back seat and began going through their provisions. There were cans of tuna and pressed ham, some granola bars, flat bread, dates, a bag of oranges, three gallon jugs of water. Enough to last for a couple of days. But if they didn't find a town, or if Kumar didn't find them, they'd be in serious trouble. He'd have to ration what they ate and drank, at least for himself and Jenny. The kid was small. He'd get dehydrated fast.

Mike peeled an orange and handed it to Tim, then peeled another one for Jenny.

"We're going to have to start soon," he told her when she passed him a section of her orange. "It'll be hot in another hour. We want to get as far as we can before it does."

"Which way do we go?"

He took the compass out of his pocket. "East," he said. "Toward Zagora."

"But that…" Jenny wet her lips. "It was a two-day drive. We can't walk that far."

"With any luck we won't have to. Kumar's out looking for us. All we have to do is keep going."

She put her hand on Timmie's head as though to protect him. She'd taken him away from his father, but by doing so she'd put his life in jeopardy. She'd wanted… *She'd* wanted. Had she thought only of herself? Had she been selfish in her desire to have him with her? So selfish that she had been willing to risk his life?

She watched Mike fill the three canteens with water from one of the jugs, then, with his belt, he made a strap so that he could carry two of the jugs over his shoulder.

Two jugs of water. Three canteens. How long would it last?

"Give me your other scarf," he said, and when she did, he put the food in it and tied it with a knot.

"I can carry that." She took the scarf from him.

"You sure?"

She forced a smile. "Of course."

He handed her one of the canteens and slung the other two over his shoulder. He folded the tarp and fastened it into a makeshift backpack with two sticks he found in the back of the Jeep. He still had his gun strapped around his waist, but he needed more bullets, and so he took them, along with the extra rifle.

"Okay," he said to Timmie. "We're going to start walking."

The boy looked out over the sea of endless sand. His chin trembled. He looked at his mother, then at Mike, and shook his head. Before he could say anything, Mike swung him up out of the Jeep.

"I don't wanna go," Tim protested, but Mike, with a firm hand on the boy's shoulder, led him a little way apart. He knelt down and looked him square in the eye. "Walking in the desert is going to be real hard," he said, "especially for your mom. You and I are going to have to take care of her."

Timmie looked at Mike, his small face serious. "Because she's a girl," he said.

"That's right. I know you're a little kid, but I bet you can act pretty grown-up when you have to."

"Sure I can," Timmie said. "I can carry one of those water things, too."

"Oh, okay. Right." Mike stood and, taking one of the canteens off his shoulder, put it over Timmie's shoulder. "Let's go back for your mom now. And remember, we have to keep an eye on her and help her all we can. Got it?"

"Yes, sir."

"My name's Mike. How about calling me that? I mean, since we're a couple of guys taking care of your mom."

"'Kay," Tim said.

They went back to Jenny. "We're ready." Mike lifted her out of the Jeep. He held her for a moment. She looked at him and he tightened his hands on her shoulders. When he let her go, he vowed that somehow, some way, he would keep her and her son safe.

By noon the temperature was over a hundred and twenty. Jenny's head was covered by the black scarf, Tim's by a strip of material Mike had torn from the bottom of Jenny's robe. He'd taken off his own shirt and wrapped it around his head.

But none of them had protection enough. Both Jenny's and Tim's faces were red; he knew they were suffering.

When at last he saw an overhang of rocks, he said, "Come on. We'll rest for a while." And when they reached the rocks, he stretched the tarp from it and secured it with the two sticks he'd brought from the Jeep.

The three of them sat under it. He peeled oranges for Jenny and Tim and gave them each a drink of water from one of the canteens before he himself drank.

"Try to get some sleep," he told them.

"In this heat?" Jenny groaned, then with a smile said, "Whine, whine, whine."

"You're entitled." He looked at the boy. "How're you doing?" he asked.

"I'm hot."

"I know, kid." Mike took his shirt off his head and, wetting the tail with a little of the water from the canteen, bathed Tim's face. "Feel good?"

"Uh-huh."

Jenny watched them, puzzled. Last night Mike had been rough with the boy. Today he'd softened a bit, but it bothered her that he'd never called Timmie by his name, that he was either "kid" or "boy." Last night Timmie had been afraid of him. She didn't think he was now, but he was still being cautious. He'd trudged along through the sand this morning, and once she'd asked, "Would you like me to carry you for a while?" Before Timmie could answer, Mike had said, "He's big enough to walk."

So Timmie had trudged on, small sandaled feet sinking in the sand with each step, his face red with exertion. She'd been furious with Mike. How dare he treat her son like that? How dare he snarl at him the way he had last night? Timmie was *her* son; she'd carry him if she wanted to.

Now he said to Tim, "You and your mom try to sleep. We're going to rest here for a couple of hours before we go on."

She lay back on the sand and Timmie lay beside her. "I'm hot," he whispered.

"I know, sweetheart." She kissed his dirty face and put her arm around him. In a little while he closed his eyes and slept.

Mike looked down at the two of them. This was hard on the kid. He was a sturdy little boy, but that's what he was—a little boy. Heat like this killed men. What would it do to a child?

He thought the boy was still afraid of him, but he couldn't help that, he'd never been comfortable around kids. He didn't know what to do with them, how to talk to them. This was Jenny's son—that should make a difference, but it didn't.

He rested back on his elbows and watched the heat waves shimmer up from the rolling dunes. Maybe it was because of his own childhood, he thought. Maybe that's why he instinctively pulled away from kids. He didn't want to be like his father. The thought of ever striking a child, of taking a belt to somebody who was so little and helpless, made him sick to his stomach.

That's the way it had been for him when he was Tim's age. From the time he could remember until the time he'd left home, his father had beaten the crap out of him.

The abused become abusers, he'd read somewhere. They took out the anger they felt for the parent who had abused them on their own kids. What if he was like that? The thought chilled him.

He'd known from the day Jenny had walked into his office in Vegas that she had a son. He'd known, but in a strange sort of way, it hadn't really dawned on him that her son was a part of her. They were a package deal: Jenny and Timmie. Timmie and Jenny. He'd fallen in love with her. If they got out of this alive, he wanted to marry her. But—and it was a pretty damn big but—he didn't know how he felt about the kid.

He looked at them. Tim had curled up close to her; she had a protective arm around him. They looked alike, the same tilt of nose, the same determined chin. Mother and son, peas in a pod. He wasn't sure he could handle it.

He let them sleep an hour and a half before he touched Jenny's shoulder and said, "We'd better get going."

She sat up and rubbed her eyes. "I was dreaming about a chocolate soda and a cold shower," she said. "Trying to decide which one I wanted first."

"Your face is dirty—you'd better settle for the shower."

"Don't I wish." She sighed, then turned to her son and said, "Timmie? Wake up, Timmie. We have to go now."

Like her, he sat up and rubbed his eyes. "It's awful hot," he said.

"Awful," she agreed. "But in a couple of hours the sun will go down and it will be cooler."

"I'm kinda hungry."

Mike gave him a handful of dates and a drink from the canteen. The kid's face was still red, and in spite of the nap, he looked exhausted. When he finished the dates and they were ready to leave, Mike reached down and swung him up onto his shoulders.

"You ride for a while," he said. "When I get tired, you'll carry me. Okay?"

The kid laughed. It was a good sound.

That night they camped in the lee of a sand dune. It had been a rough day. As soon as they stopped, Jenny and the boy wanted to sleep. He wouldn't let them. He opened one of the cans of tuna and one of pressed meat, and cut slices of the flat bread.

The boy could barely keep his eyes open. "C'mon, kid," Mike said. "Chow time."

"I'm not hungry."

"Sure, you are." Mike put some tuna on one of the plastic forks. "Open up," he ordered.

Tim did as he was told. After the first two bites, he admitted it was pretty good, took the fork and started to eat by himself.

Jenny watched the play between them. Mike was being tough. She didn't like that. Timmie was only a little boy, a scared little boy who had once again been thrust into a strange environment. He hadn't seen her in more than six months; he'd never seen Mike before. He'd been terrorized last night, exposed to gunfire and to a terrible storm. Today had been an inferno of heat, and tomorrow would be worse.

Mike should have understood that. He was gentle with her; why couldn't he be the same with her son?

She didn't know how long they could go on this way, but she did know that as long as there was strength in her body, she would protect Timmie. She would go until she dropped and then, because she'd have no other choice, she would entrust her son to Mike. In spite of his brusqueness and his toughness, he would fight to save her son, she knew.

When they had eaten, Mike found a few pieces of scrub and made a small fire with the twigs. He stretched the tarp out on the sand, and Tim curled up close to Jenny and went to sleep.

"He's a pretty good kid," Mike said.

"He has a name."

Mike looked at her, surprised.

"His name is Tim. Not *kid,* not *boy*— Tim."

"Okay. Sorry. I guess I'm not used to kids. I guess I'm not very good with them."

"Why?"

He looked at her across the fire. His eyebrows drew together, then he shrugged. "No special reason."

"I think there is. Tell me."

He'd never told anybody—not the teachers who asked about his bruises, not the welfare worker who'd come to the house and found him with a lump on the side of his face as big as a golf ball. He'd been too ashamed of the way they lived and of the drunken father who'd vented his rage on his only son to tell anybody.

"Mike?" Jenny moved closer, concerned by the way his face had gone still when she'd asked him, by the glimmer of remembered pain in his eyes. "What is it?" she asked softly. "You can tell me, Mike. You can tell me anything."

"My father was a drunk," he said. "Every time he drank he beat the hell out of me." He stared down into the fire. "Maybe that's why I'm not good with kids. With Tim. I can see myself at his age and it scares the hell out of me."

"But why? Why would that scare you?"

"What if I..." He looked at her from across the fire. "Maybe if I had a kid, I'd be like my father," he said in a voice so low she could barely hear.

She sucked in her breath, wanting to touch him. Afraid to touch him.

"I love you," he said. "I don't think I've ever said it before, Jenny, but I do. Love you. I want to spend every minute of the rest of my life with you."

She waited. When he didn't say anything, she said, "But?"

He took a deep breath. "But I'm not ready to be a full-time father. I might never be ready."

For a moment Jenny was silent. Then she said, "I see."

"Maybe in time..." He looked at her, then away. "I'm sorry, Jen, but I just don't think I'm ready to take on fatherhood."

There it was, flat out. End of discussion. I love you but I'm afraid I'll never love your son. There was nothing else to say...except, "I'm tired, Mike. I'm going to sleep now."

"Okay." He cleared his throat. "We're going to start out before dawn. I'll wake you."

"You'd better get some sleep, too." She lay down next to Timmie and turned her back to Mike.

He felt empty, depleted. He stared into the fire and saw the images of his childhood. His frightened mother cowering in a corner when his father took his belt off and began to hit him. In the crackle of flames he heard her sobs, the grunt of effort each time his father struck him. His own anguished cries.

And somewhere in the back of his mind was the terrible thought, What if I'm like him? What if I'm like him?

They left two hours before dawn. The canteens were full, and they had one jug of water left. Tim walked beside Jenny, holding her hand, stumbling through the darkness. Once the boy said, "I'm tired. My legs hurt."

"C'mon, kid, you can walk," Mike told him.

He felt like a marine drill sergeant ordering his men on a forced march. Only these weren't men, they were a woman and a small boy.

They had to go on, had to cover as much ground as they could before the sun rose, before the desert became an inferno of heat. By the light of a flashlight he checked the compass. Due east. Keep going.

The sun came up, a great ball of red in the east. The sky turned from gray to pink, casting shadows of light on the golden dunes. It was beautiful. And oh, so deadly.

They stopped for a ten-minute rest. He gave Jenny and the boy an orange and took one for himself. There were only two left. When they started out again, he put the boy on his shoulders.

Jenny had little to say. It was as though she had already moved somehow apart from him—she and the boy, mother and son, removed from him, a stranger.

By one that afternoon the desert floor was a blaze of heat. They stopped to drink the last of the water in Jenny's canteen.

Before they started out again he scanned the horizon, looking for something, anything—any sign of life. But there was nothing, only the rise and fall of mile after endless mile of sand.

Once the boy cried out, "Water! I see water!" But when Mike peered out at the shimmering heat, he knew it was only a mirage.

Jenny walked on without complaint, but now and then she stumbled. Each time she did, she said, "Sorry, sorry," as though she'd done something wrong.

Time and again Mike looked up at the sky, hoping to see a bird, something that might indicate they were close to a village or an oasis. But there was nothing, only this vast wasteland of sand. And the sun, hot, relentless, beating them down.

The next time Jenny stumbled, he called a halt and rigged up the tarp. He gave both Jenny and the boy a drink from the canteen, but they were too exhausted to eat, and lay where they were, under the tarp, mouths open, gasping for air.

In a little while he lay down beside them, and when he reached for Jenny's hand, she entwined her fingers with his.

"We're not going to make it, are we, Mike?" she whispered.

"Sure," he said. "Sure, we're going to. We'll find something soon, a village...something." He raised himself up on one elbow and looked down at her. Her face was dirty, her lips blistered. He loved her.

"Promise me," she said.

"Anything."

"I don't think I'm going to make it. You're stronger than I am. You might."

That scared him. He didn't want to talk about it. "Aw, c'mon, Jen," he said.

"I know we're low on water, that probably we need more than we're drinking. I'm not going to drink any more. I want you and Tim to have it. And if I can't keep up..."

Fear roughened his voice. "What in the hell are you talking about?"

"I want you to leave me," she said. "I want you and Tim to go on. If you make it, take him to my parents in Ramona. Tell them I love them. Tell them—"

"Shut up!" he said viciously. "Just shut the hell up." Then, because he couldn't help himself, he gathered her in his arms and held her as though he would never let her go.

"We're going to make it," he said against her blistered lips. "I swear to you, Jenny, we're going to make it."

And prayed to God and to Allah that it was true.

Chapter 16

Jenny had been staggering for the last hour. When she fell, Mike put the boy down and went to her. She clung to him and he saw the desperation in her eyes.

The boy was weakening, too. For the last hour he'd barely managed to hang on to the top of Mike's head.

Mike gave them each a drink of water. Jenny tried to refuse. "No," she protested weakly, "give it to Tim."

He didn't listen, but held the canteen to her mouth and made her drink. They rested, holding the tarp over their heads for what little shade it offered. But in a little while he got them up and forced them to go on.

He didn't think they'd make it through another day. Jenny could barely put one foot ahead of the other. Still she kept on, looking like a desert woman in the black robe and head scarf. But she wasn't a desert woman. She belonged in a place that was clean and cool, where she could eat all of the ice-cream sodas she wanted to.

She was beautiful. Courageous. Sexy. Yeah, sexy as hell. Making love with her had been the most, the best. He wanted her beside him every night for the rest of his life. To sleep with her, wake with her, make love with her. Love...

His mind wandered with strangely erotic thoughts. Jenny covered with chocolate ice cream, while slowly, inch by delicious inch, he licked it off her body...

Jenny naked, splashing in green ocean waves, beckoning to him like a siren from the sea...

Jenny coming to him up out of the pool, like that night in Death Valley—her body glistening wet, cool and sleek against his. Water dripping off her breasts...

Water...

He closed his eyes and tried to lick his dry, cracked lips, and when he opened them he saw water shimmering in the sunlight and he wanted to laugh because it was only a mirage, because the palm trees were some kind of crazy prop.

They're trying to fool you, he told himself. The gods are laughing at you, Brennan. Ignore 'em. Just keep on going, one step at a time. Forget the mirage. It's only...

He stopped, staring out with blurry eyes, then a sob rose in his throat and he cried, "Jenny! Jenny, look!"

Her eyes were so dazed she could barely focus. "What?" she mumbled. "What is it?"

He pointed to the right. "Water," he croaked. "An oasis."

"Oh," she said, and fell unconscious in the sand before he could reach her.

He put the boy down. He picked Jenny up and put her over his shoulder. Then he took the boy's hand and together they staggered toward the oasis.

He kept talking, telling her and the boy that they were almost there.

"Everything's okay," he said. "We made it. We're okay. Okay. Okay."

Tim stumbled. Mike tightened his hold on the kid's hand and half walked, half dragged him through the sand.

Thirty yards, twenty... Shade under the trees. Take 'em there, next to the pool. C'mon, Brennan. You can do it. Do it for them. For Jenny. For the kid.

He laid her down and dragged Tim forward. The water was clean, cool. He splashed it on the boy and cupped more in his hand for him to drink before he turned to scoop handfuls of it over Jenny.

She opened her eyes. "No," she mumbled. "Give it to Tim."

He held her up, supporting her with his arm, and cupping water in his other hand, held it to her lips. "Drink all you want," he said. "We have enough. We've found an oasis."

"An oasis?"

"Yeah." He tried to smile, but his lips were cracked and it hurt too much.

"Where's Tim? Is he all right?" Her voice was weak; she could barely speak. "Where is he?"

Mike pointed. Tim was on his belly, drinking from the pool. "He's okay," he said, and pulled the black robe over her head.

"Don't," she protested. "You mustn't. Tim—"

He didn't listen. Both she and the boy were dehydrated. He had to get them into the water. He picked her up and with the last bit of his strength lowered her into the pool.

"Ohh," she said, forgetting to be angry. "Ohh, this feels good."

"You, too, boy." He motioned to him. "C'mere." And when Tim approached, Mike took his sandals off and stripped him. "Get into the water with your mom," he said.

Tim waded in and plopped down in the shallow water close to his mother. For a little while he only sat there, then he said, "Your face is dirty, Mama."

"So's yours," she answered. Then she put her arms around him and started to cry.

Mike watched the two of them, then lay on his belly as Tim had done and drank his fill.

He hadn't thought they'd make it. He'd told himself that tonight would be the last night; that in the morning he'd have to tell them there was no point in going on.

He wouldn't have to do that now, because there was hope. They were all right, at least for a little while. There was a spring that poured fresh water into the pool, and dates when they ran out of food. Maybe Kumar knew about the oasis. If he did, he'd find them. All they had to do was hold out until then.

He took his boots off, then peeled down to his shorts and waded into the water.

Jenny smiled up at him. She was still weak, still a little dazed, but she could smile. "Thank you for taking care of us, Mike," she said. "Thank you for getting us here."

"We're going to be all right now, Jen."

"Yes, I know."

Then there were no more words. They were content just to lie still and feel the water cool their skin, soak-

ing into their pores. Once in a while Timmie splashed
the surface with the flat of his hand, but even he was
quiet.

The sun lowered and the sky turned from blue to
patterned shades of pink, flamingo, then yellow
streaked with green, and finally a darkening, brilliant
red. The sand was gold, the dune beyond shadowed in
amber and mauve. The desert at twilight.

At last they came out of the water. Jenny put her
robe on over her bra and panties, but Timmie didn't.

Naked as a sprite in the last light of the day, he
looked smaller, somehow more vulnerable. Something clutched at Mike's insides. How could anybody
ever hurt a little kid like that? Tim weighed what—
Maybe forty-five pounds to his own two-ten? The idea
of anyone his size hurting anyone Tim's size was in-
conceivable. Yet his father had hurt him. And the
thought of it was like a poison in his blood.

He turned away, as much from them as from the
emotion welling up inside him. He spread the tarp, and
when he'd laid out the food, told them to come and
eat.

They had pressed ham for dinner, which they ate out
of the can. Dessert was a granola bar split three ways,
and as many dates as they could eat.

By the time they finished, Tim was nodding.

"Bedtime," he told the boy.

"I want Mama to come, too."

"Your mom's right here. She'll be with you in a little while."

The small chin was thrust out. "But I want her to
come now!"

"Dammit, kid..."

The chin started to tremble.

Mike reached for the boy and put his arm around him. "I'm sorry I yelled at you, kiddo. We've all had a rough time and I guess I'm grouchy. And you're right—your mom is pretty tired. It's her bedtime, too." He ruffled the boy's hair. Then he put his arms around Jenny and kissed her.

The kid looked startled. Jenny looked embarrassed. Mike didn't say anything.

Mother and son lay down together. When they were asleep, Mike leaned back against one of the date palms and wished he had a cigarette. It was early evening now, quiet, with only the faintest of breezes rustling the palm fronds. He could smell the desert, and the water, and thanked God for the miracle that had led them here.

They couldn't stay forever, but he was pretty sure they could hold out until help came. Kumar would be searching for them. If he didn't find them, there was a chance that a passing caravan of desert nomads would. They had enough canned food to last a couple of days. After that they could subsist, at least for a little while, on water and dates.

He fell asleep with his back against the palm, but later, when he awoke, he crawled over to the tarp where Jenny and the boy slept, and lying down beside them, went back to sleep.

Tim spent most of the time in the water, splashing contentedly as though he couldn't get enough of it. He and Mike were alone in the pool for a few minutes the next day while Jenny napped under the shade of the palms, and Tim asked, "How come you kissed Mama?"

"Because I like her," Mike said.

"You're not married to her—she's married to my father."

Mike shook his head. "No, Tim. They used to be married, but they're not any more."

"Is that why my father took me away?"

"Probably."

"Don't my mother and my father like each other?"

"Well," Mike said, stalling for time while he tried to find the right words. "Well, sometimes things happen between grown-ups. Most of the time it isn't anybody's fault. They just don't get along, and when that happens, they decide to separate, like your mom and dad did. But that doesn't mean they don't love you. Both your mom and your dad love you a lot. Your mom came all the way from California because she loves you so much."

"But my dad is still my dad, right?"

"Right." Mike hesitated. "Were you happy living here in Jahan with your father?"

"Sometimes. Lots of stuff was different, you know? Like the food was real strange. And I had to wear a robe instead of pants." He looked down at the water, snapped at it with his thumb and third finger and watched the ripples. "My dad's okay, but I don't like my uncle Mustafa." He lowered his voice, as though afraid Jenny might hear. "If I said words in English, he'd hit me. I don't ever want to go back where he is."

Mike nodded. "Yeah," he said. "I understand. And I've got news for you, kid. You're not going back. He's not going to hit you anymore and neither is anybody else."

Timmie looked at Mike. "You sure?"

"Damn right I'm sure."

The kid took a deep breath. Then he grinned. "We're going away," he said. "In a big airplane. To where Grandma and Grandpa are. Right?"

"Right as right." Mike scooped up a handful of water and poured it over Tim's head. "That's exactly what we're going to do. Just as soon as we get out of here."

They heard the plane the next morning. It banked low over the oasis, and when it did, Mike grabbed Tim's white robe and ran out from the shelter of the trees to the sand where he could be spotted. It banked again, then flew away.

"Will they come back?" Jenny cried. "Do you think it was Kumar?"

"Yeah, either Kumar or a scout plane he sent out. They won't be able to land here. What they'll probably do is signal to the search party." He took her hand and squeezed it. "By tonight we'll be in Zagora eating shish kebab with Kumar."

"Can I have a hamburger?" Tim asked.

"You can have anything you want, boy." Mike picked him up and swung him over his head. "Any damn thing you want."

He hoped the search party wasn't too far away, hoped it would find them before dark. Now that somebody had spotted them, it'd be hard waiting. He wanted Jenny and the boy to be where he'd know with absolute certainty they were safe. Besides, he needed a shave.

It was late afternoon when they heard the sound of hooves. "Horses!" Mike yelled. "They're coming up over the dune." He waved his arms, yelling as soon as he saw them, even though he knew they couldn't hear him.

"Hey!" he cried. "Here we are! Here we are!" And, too excited to stand still, he started to run toward them.

"Wait!" Jenny said. "Mike, wait!"

He swung around.

"It's not..." Her eyes went wide with horror. "Oh, God!" she cried. "It's them! Aiden! Mustafa!"

He peered through the cloud of dust rising from the galloping hooves, trying to distinguish the men astride them. Burnooses flapping, black and white *howlis* all but covering their faces, they approached steadily. But even covered as they were, he knew Jenny was right. It wasn't Kumar and his men. It was Mustafa, Aiden, the old man and three other riders. Coming hell-bent at them.

He ran for the gun, grabbed it and strapped the holster with the extra bullets around his waist before he picked up the rifle.

"You and Tim get behind a tree," he shouted. "Stay down."

"No!" Jenny snatched the rifle away from him, then, grasping her son's hand, ran with him to one of the date palms.

Timmie's eyes were wide with fear. "It's Uncle Mustafa!" he cried.

"Yes," she said tightly. "It's Uncle Mustafa." She felt strangely calm and unafraid. The man she hated had come to try to take her son away from her. She knew with absolute certainty that she would kill him before she let that happen.

They came closer, horses' hooves flying, kicking up the sand. They gave a terrible, primitive cry and raised their rifles above their heads, running hard toward the oasis.

Jenny raised her weapon, sighted and aimed at the man nearest her.

"Closer," she whispered. "Closer." Her finger tightened on the trigger. She pulled, and with a high-pitched scream, the rider fell.

But still they came, so close she could smell horse sweat and man sweat. She raised up to fire again, sighted, and looked into Mustafa's eyes, eyes that were narrowed with hate.

With a bansheelike cry that was straight out of hell, he wheeled his horse and came straight at her.

Steady, she told herself. Steady...

Tim screamed, a scream of pure terror. Before Jenny could stop him, he was up and running, running away from the man he so feared.

"Timmie!" she cried. "Come back!"

Mustafa saw the boy running toward the water. He hesitated, then yanked his horse around and went after Tim.

Timmie ran on, eyes wide with fear as he looked back over his shoulder.

Mustafa bore down on him, reached low and swept the boy up onto the horse. "I have him!" he cried to his men. "*Balak!* Move out."

Mike brought down a man. He aimed for another, heard Jenny scream and saw Mustafa galloping toward her. Before he could fire, Mustafa had turned and was riding toward the pond. As though in slow motion Mike saw the kid, small legs pumping in an effort to get away. Then Mustafa, leaning low from the saddle, scooping the boy up in front of him.

Mike raised his gun, tried to sight. But he couldn't take a chance on hitting the kid.

"Timmie!" he cried, then he was up and running straight at the horse.

Mustafa saw him. With a cry of rage he wheeled his mount and ran at Mike as though to run him down.

Mike stood his ground, too filled with fear for the boy to be cautious. The horse raced toward him. He jumped to the side and grabbed the reins. The horse reared. He hung on and yanked hard on the horse's head. It reared again, and when it stamped back to the sand, Mike grabbed Tim and swung him to the ground.

"Run!" he cried. Then he reached for Mustafa and dragged him off the horse.

He smashed his fist into Mustafa's face. A knife flashed out. They went down, struggling, panting with effort and with rage. Mustafa slashed again and Mike felt the burn as the knife cut into his wrist. He hit Mustafa with his bloody hand, a red glaze of fury in his eyes because he wanted to kill the man who had hurt Jenny and her boy. The knife struck again, cutting deep into his shoulder. He fell back, weakened, and felt Mustafa's hands close on his throat in a vise-like grip.

Mike thrust his body upward, struggling against the blackness that threatened. With the last bit of his strength, he clasped his fists together and struck Mustafa across the throat. He heard the crunch of bone. Mustafa gasped and fell back on the sand.

Mike staggered to his knees. Above the noise of sporadic gunfire he heard a roaring sound in his ears, and Jenny calling out to him.

He looked at her, dazed, disoriented. "What?" he said. "What?"

She pointed upward. "Look!" she cried.

And when he did he saw the copter.

A cry went up among the men who were left. *"Balak! Balak!"* they shouted. "Move out! Get away!"

They wheeled their horses and galloped for the dune. There were three left: Aiden, his father, another man.

The copter stirred up the sand, making it hard to see. Jenny ran to Tim and picked him up in her arms. Mike stood above Mustafa's body and looked toward the horsemen fleeing toward the dune.

He picked up his rifle and took aim. His finger was on the trigger; he had only to squeeze. They were still within firing range. He could... No, he couldn't. One of those men was Tim's father. He couldn't do it.

At the top of the dune one of the horsemen stopped. He turned his mount and looked back at the oasis. Then he raised his arm as though in farewell, and disappeared down the other side.

"We've been looking for you for three days." Kumar jumped out of the copter and ran toward Mike. "Thank Allah we arrived in time. Are you...?" He saw the blood running down Mike's arm. And Mustafa, facedown in the sand.

"He is dead, yes?"

"Yeah." Mike shook his head, trying to clear it. "I don't want the boy to see him."

"My men will take care of it and I will take care of you. You've got a couple of nasty wounds, Mike. Come." He took Mike's arm and led him to where Jenny was standing with her son.

"Hello, Kumar." She looked at Mike and, without a word, still holding Timmie, put an arm around him and held him close.

"It's over," he said.

"Yes." A sigh trembled through her and she let him go.

He took the boy from her. "Are you all right?" he asked. "Did I hurt you when I pulled you off the horse?"

Timmie shook his head. There was a scratch on his cheek and sand in his hair. "He—he was going to take me away," he whispered.

"But we didn't let him, did we?" He put his arms around the boy. "Nobody's ever going to hurt you again." He held the little body close. "Not ever again," he said.

Timmie hung on. "He hurt you," he whispered.

"Nah." Mike put him down. "But I guess I'd better let my friend here take care of it. Tim, this is Kumar Ben Ari. He's going to fly us out of here in his copter. How would you like that?"

Tim's eyes went wide. He looked toward the whirlybird. "I'm going to ride in that?"

"Yep." Mike ruffled the kid's hair. "And your mom and I will be with you. Okay?"

Jenny took the boy to the other side of the pool while Kumar bandaged Mike's arm and his wrist. She could hear the snick of a small shovel against sand, and knew Kumar's men were burying Mustafa and the others who had been shot. She, too, had seen Aiden from the top of the sand dune, and now she silently thanked Allah that he had not been killed. He was Tim's father. She didn't know if either of them would ever see him again, but she was glad he lived.

In a little while Kumar called out, "We're ready. Everybody into the copter."

He helped Jenny in. Tim came next, then Mike.

The rotors started. Timmie looked a little nervous. He turned to Mike, not liking the noise.

Mike reached for him and pulled him onto his lap.

"Don't let go!" Timmie said.

Mike tightened his good arm around the boy as the copter lifted. "I won't, Tim." He looked over the boy's head at Jenny. "Not ever," he said.

They'd flown out of Jahan on Kumar's private plane, and for the past week they had been recuperating in his home in Abdu Resaba.

The house in Zagora had been luxurious; this place was a king's palace. Jenny and Tim had a suite with a bedroom for each of them. Mike's suite was next to theirs.

On the night before they were to leave on the return trip to California, the four of them had dinner on the terrace. Timmie had a hamburger and French fries, the adults had a typical Middle-Eastern meal. A meal interspersed with gunfire.

"Target practice," Kumar explained with a smile. "The army post is down in the city, but when the wind is in our direction the sound carries up here. I'm afraid there will be other disturbances as well, but pay no attention. It is only practice warfare."

He passed more french fries to Timmie. "I'm going to miss you," he told Mike and Jenny. "I hope the three of you will return for a visit."

The three of them. Jenny and Mike had not been alone since that night before she had gone to the Huranis' house. On the desert he had told her he wasn't ready for fatherhood. Had he changed? she wondered.

He was very good with Tim now, even calling him by name instead of "kid" or "boy." And Tim liked him—she could see that. But she still didn't know what was going to happen when they returned to California.

When the hour grew late, she took Timmie's hand and they said good-night to the two men. She put Tim to bed, and when he was asleep, she went out to the patio that opened off her room and gazed out on the desert night.

So much had happened since the day she had walked into Mike's office in Las Vegas. Lives had been lost; she had her son back.

And she had fallen in love. Had Mike? She thought he had, but she didn't know if he was ready for the kind of commitment she wanted, a commitment that meant marriage and a life that included Timmie.

Then, through the darkness, she heard him say, "Our last night in the desert, Jenny."

He crossed from his patio to hers and, looking out at the desert night, said, "In spite of everything we've been through, there's a part of me that doesn't want to leave. I—"

Suddenly an explosion of sound shattered the night. The earth beneath their feet shook and the sky caught fire in a brilliance of bright orange flame.

She said, "What...?" And the next thing she knew she was flat on the ground and Mike was on top of her, shielding her with his body.

"What's happening?" she cried.

"I don't know. Stay down!... Oh *hell*! It's a practice attack. Kumar told us at dinner." He seemed embarrassed, and said, "Sorry. I thought it was real. Did I hurt you?" He shifted and started to get up.

Jenny shook her head. "No, you didn't hurt me." She looked up at him. "Where're you going? There might be another explosion at any minute."

He grinned. "In that case maybe I'd better stay right here."

"I think that would be a good idea." His face was only inches from hers. "It's okay if you want to kiss me . . . or anything."

"Anything?"

"You bet."

His expression changed. He kissed her and when the kiss ended he said, "I love you, Jenny. I love your son and I'll love the children we'll have together." He kissed her again and felt her body soften under his. "Will you marry me, Jen? Will you be my wife and stay with me forever?"

"Oh, Mike," she said. "Oh, yes."

They held each other while the glow of orange faded from the sky and the night became dark again. At last he said, "I'd better let you up."

"Not yet." She cupped his face between her two hands. "Not quite yet, Brennan."

"Ah, Jen." He rained kisses over her face, on her forehead, her eyes, her cheeks. He kissed her mouth and when the kiss deepened they joined their bodies one to the other and made love there in the quiet desert night.

It was a coupling both gentle and fierce. In the final glorious moment he whispered her name and said, "Love me, Jenny mine. Please love me."

"Forever," she said. And knew in her heart that she would.

* * * * *

HE'S AN

AMERICAN HERO

January 1994 rings in the New Year—and a new lineup of sensational American Heroes. You can't seem to get enough of these men, and we're proud to feature one each month, created by some of your favorite authors.

January: CUTS BOTH WAYS by Dee Holmes: Erin Kenyon hired old acquaintance Ashe Seager to investigate the crash that claimed her husband's life, only to learn old memories never die.

February: A WANTED MAN by Kathleen Creighton: Mike Lanagan's exposé on corruption earned him accolades...and the threat of death. Running for his life, he found sanctuary in the arms of Lucy Brown—but for how long?

March: COOPER by Linda Turner: Cooper Rawlings wanted nothing to do with the daughter of the man who'd shot his brother. But when someone threatened Susannah Patterson's life, he found himself riding to the rescue....

AMERICAN HEROES: Men who give all they've got for their country, their work—the women they love.

Only from

Take 4 bestselling love stories FREE

Plus get a FREE surprise gift!

ROMANTIC TRADITIONS

Paula Detmer Riggs kicks off ROMANTIC TRADITIONS this month with **ONCE UPON A WEDDING (IM #524)**, which features a fresh spin on the marriage-of-convenience motif. Jesse Dante married Hazel O'Connor to help an orphaned baby, underestimating the powers of passion and parenthood....

Coming to stores in January will be bestselling author Marilyn Pappano's **FINALLY A FATHER (IM #542)**, spotlighting the time-honored secret-baby story line. Quin Ellis had lied about her daughter's real parentage for over nine years. But Mac McEwen's return to town signaled an end to her secret.

In April, expect an innovative look at the amnesia plot line in Carla Cassidy's **TRY TO REMEMBER**.

And ROMANTIC TRADITIONS doesn't stop there! In months to come we'll be bringing you more classic plot lines told the Intimate Moments way. So, if you're the romantic type who appreciates tradition with a twist, come experience ROMANTIC TRADITIONS—only in

SIMRT2

And now for
something completely different
from Silhouette....

SPELLBOUND
R O M A N C E

Unique and innovative stories that take you into the world of paranormal happenings. Look for our special "Spellbound" flash—and get ready for a truly exciting reading experience!

**In February, look for
One Unbelievable Man (SR #993)
by Pat Montana.**

Was he man or myth? Cass Kohlmann's mysterious traveling companion, Michael O'Shea, had her all confused. He'd suddenly appeared, claiming she was his destiny—determined to win her heart. But could levelheaded Cass learn to believe in fairy tales...before her fantasy man disappeared forever?

Don't miss the charming, sexy and utterly mysterious
Michael O'Shea in
ONE UNBELIEVABLE MAN.
Watch for him in February—only from

Silhouette
R O M A N C E™

As seen on TV!
Free Gift Offer

With a Free Gift proof-of-purchase from any Silhouette® book, you can receive a beautiful cubic zirconia pendant.

This gorgeous marquise-shaped stone is a genuine cubic zirconia—accented by an 18" gold tone necklace.

(Approximate retail value $19.95)

Send for yours today...
compliments of ▼ *Silhouette®*
™

Free Gift Certificate

Name: _____

Address: _____

City: _____ State/Province: _____ Zip/Postal Code: _____

Mail this certificate, one proof-of-purchase and a check or money order for postage and handling to: SILHOUETTE FREE GIFT OFFER 1994. In the U.S.: 3010 Walden Avenue, P.O. Box 9057, Buffalo NY 14269-9057. In Canada: P.O. Box 622, Fort Erie, Ontario L2Z 5X3